THE HOBBY

CAROLYN FAULKNER

Published by Blushing Books
An Imprint of
ABCD Graphics and Design, Inc.
A Virginia Corporation
977 Seminole Trail #233
Charlottesville, VA 22901

The Hobby
Carolyn Faulkner

EBook ISBN:
Print ISBN:

Chapter 1

SHE STARTED at the knock on the door, although she had no real right to, since it was hardly unexpected.

Early bird that she was, she'd been sitting there for quite some time, in various tense and uncomfortable positions, moving from the easy chair to the pseudo-office chair to the couch, then back to the easy chair, and even occasionally, motivated by her own sheer nervousness to actually pace back and forth in front of the window. And anyone who looked at her would immediately know that pacing wasn't something she did very often.

Brielle Daley rose from her tentative perch on the window sill and headed to the door, wondering with every step what the hell it was that she thought she was doing.

Sooner than she wanted, she arrived there, in time to hear a slightly more insistent round of knocks.

Taking several steps away—although she couldn't have said why—she said, "I'm here. Just a sec."

Straightening her comfortable, sensible ensemble of a non-descript blouse and skirt—topped off with a pair of shoes that looked like they could have belonged to her nana

—she smoothed imaginary wrinkles out of her outfit and again stood in front of the door. She felt as if she were a schoolgirl who had been sent to the principal for some kind of infraction.

But she wouldn't really know how that felt, since she had been a model student—a brown noser of the highest order, frankly; ever eager to please—and had never once been subject to any kind of discipline during any of her school years.

And if that scenario were true, she would be the one knocking on his door.

Standing there perseverating about things like that wasn't helping her any—if anything, it was making her feel even more nervous than she had before. So she forced herself to take a breath, look through the peephole, flick the little ball-catchy thingy above the handle, and open the door.

He was standing there in a suit that looked like it cost more than her condo, but then she knew that couldn't be the case. She didn't think gigolos made that kind of money— although she could be wrong.

And the briefcase he was holding had definitely seen better days.

Still, he'd managed—by simply appearing there, where she'd contracted for him to be—to make her feel like a dowdy old maid. Bri didn't know what she thought he'd wear to this weird meeting of theirs, but she guessed it wasn't a suit.

"Hello, Jennifer," he said smoothly. It was kind of jarring to hear that name in reference to herself, but she was more than smart enough not to use her real name in that kind of situation.

She'd always loved a British accent, having seen every possible period drama the BBC and its affiliates ever offered. She hadn't seen that noted on his profile, which was surprising. It certainly would have been a selling point for her and a lot of other women, too, she would imagine.

Normally, she found it infinitely soothing but, at the same time, incredibly sexy.

But that didn't translate to in-person, apparently.

The truth was that there was pretty much nothing that was going to calm her anxiety about what she was doing, except—perhaps—to stop doing it and send him packing.

But now that he was right there—close enough for her to smell his incredibly wonderful aftershave—she couldn't quite bring herself to say the words that would do that.

Instead, she stood there, her instantly Sahara dry mouth hanging open unbecomingly as she gaped at him. He was even more handsome than she'd thought from his picture, which merely ratcheted up her stress level from the "I might maybe survive this" to the "run for your life" level.

Without saying a word—because she didn't have the spit necessary to do so, and she'd rather not have him think that she was pre-verbal—Bri turned and headed into the room, which wasn't something she necessarily wanted to do, but if she didn't sit down quickly, she was going to faint.

She'd been pale when she'd opened the door, and she'd only grown paler—if that was even possible—in the few seconds since she'd let him in. Branson Keller followed her into the room, closing and locking the two available locks on the door before using his long legs to eat up the carpet between them, worried that he might need to catch her if she crumpled to the floor, and it looked like that was a real possibility.

She literally dropped into one of the occasional chairs, and he could see how hard she was shaking long before he got to her.

Tucking his briefcase next to the sofa, he dropped gracefully to one knee in front of her— but carefully not crowding her— asking in a calm, quiet tone, "Jenny, are you all right?"

"No!" she panted. "I don't think that I can do this!" she barely got out, drawing a ragged breath between each word.

"Let's not worry about that at the moment. I want to get you calmed down." He glanced around the room, noting that there was an honor bar, which he crossed to immediately. Upon perusing the offerings, he took a couple of the pony bottles of low priced— but somehow still outrageously expensive—whiskey. Grabbing the glass that had the pretty fluted paper cap on it, he poured the amber liquid into it and presented her with the glass.

She wasn't looking at him, but at the floor instead.

"Jenny. Take a sip of this." There was a mild hint of dominance in that order.

Her auburn head came up then went right back down again. "Oh, I don't drink."

"Because of your religion?"

"No."

"Because you're allergic?"

"No."

"Why, then?"

"Because I don't like the taste," she barely got out.

Branson grimaced. He didn't like how she was breathing and knew he needed to get her to calm down. This was the quickest method he knew.

"Then I'm not asking," he said, using a much stricter tone.

Her head snapped up as if he'd given her an electric shock, eyes locking with his.

More gently, he encouraged, "Take the glass and a healthy swallow please."

Bri found the small courtesy at the end of that order surprisingly sexy, although she wasn't sure why. He was looking at her expectantly, and for the first time in her life, she knew that there was someone in front of her who wasn't going to allow her to get away with disobeying him.

That thought was both arousing and alarming, in what were pretty equal levels, at that point.

Bri had learned early that being a good student who was able to express herself well, along with being polite and mature, allowed her to have been considered a pseudo-adult for most of her life—long before she should have, really. As an only child, she'd spent most of her time around adults, anyway, and her parents treated her more as a contemporary than their child most of the time. And as long as she showed them what they wanted to see from her, she could get away with almost anything. And if they caught on to anything, she had an almost foolproof method to handle that, too, by, essentially, admitting to her wrongdoing and throwing herself on the mercy of the court.

Luckily, she didn't really have any habits for which she could end up in real trouble. Bri rebelled a bit in high school, but smoking and staying out late was the entirety of it, since she couldn't stand the taste of alcohol then, either. She did end up skipping a lot of school in order to stay home and masturbate—once she'd discovered that wonderful ability— but she was more than capable of mimicking her mother's voice to call the attendance office as her, and she made sure to make up the work she needed to before it became a problem.

Because she was so well-behaved, her parents weren't really looking for her to do anything bad—and were just as happy not to have to—and she easily got away with the small things she wanted to do without them ever knowing she'd done them.

But the man in front of her wasn't her parent, and she knew that he wouldn't be inclined to let her get away with the things she'd been getting away with all her life. In general, she knew how to get around pretty much anyone in authority—her parents, teachers, and even bosses—by extrapolating what she'd done with her parents when she was caught out after curfew.

If she did do something wrong and it got noticed, she made a rule early on not to wait to be caught, but to walk into her dad's study—or her boss's office—and confess completely and as sincerely as she could—and apparently, that was pretty darned sincerely. She had obviously missed her calling and should have gone into acting. Doing so almost always eliminated any kind of negative repercussions that might have resulted in conjunction with her behavior.

Her parents were a little less impressed with her doing that, but then, she'd been doing it with them much longer. Bosses, however, were always nearly thunderstruck that she'd do that. And although she was enough of a detail-oriented person who was highly self-motivated to do well, so that kind of situation didn't crop up very often, her willingness to "own up" to whatever mistake she'd made was often mentioned in annual reviews, and she directly attributed several promotions and even more raises to doing that early on in her career.

It wasn't as if she was a coldly calculating person, though. She was pleasant and fun to work with, but also unafraid to take the lead and to do whatever was necessary to ensure that a project was done well, or a client was very happy with her willingness to go above and beyond to make sure that was true.

And she had more than enough friends, who had all come to count on her for a lot of belly laughs, as well as her willingness to be a caretaker to them when they needed it— and even when they didn't think they needed it. Bri was also known to be generous to a fault when someone was in need, even to the point of putting herself in a bind, although that happened less nowadays since her salary had risen commensurate with her abilities.

Bri could be scrupulously honest, too, especially with herself and her friends—perhaps even a bit too much with either of them. She was very hard on herself about a lot of things unnecessarily, and as she'd matured, although she'd continued to unhesitatingly admit when she'd screwed up, it was much less calculated than it had been when she was younger and much more heartfelt.

Guilt was a wonderful motivator.

The incredibly gorgeous man who was still on one knee before her wouldn't be susceptible to her trying to cajole, impress, or otherwise connive in any way that would change how he would decide to deal with her if she disobeyed him.

That was one of the reasons why she'd chosen him originally and stuck with him while they chatted online about possibly meeting. She barely knew him, but she knew that about him without the slightest doubt.

It was exactly what she needed—but was terrified of experiencing at the same time.

And yet here she was, alone in a hotel room, with him looking at her like that—just like she'd thought a Dom would, holding her eyes, staring up at her with a set—but not angry— look on his face as he waited the scant second that ticked by until she took the glass from him and downed the entire two fingers worth in one gulp.

That, of course, set her to coughing practically to the point of retching, and before she knew it, he was pressing a bottle of water into her hand. "Take a few small swallows. I don't fancy ending up at the ER tonight."

Without thinking, Bri did exactly as he suggested, and the coughing subsided.

"Feeling a bit better?" he asked, turning just enough to

put the empty glass on the end table but leaving the water with her.

Bri was feeling well enough to note that he continued to remain on his knees in front of her, despite the fact that that was supposedly where she would be, in most D/s fantasies.

"Yes, thank you," she croaked. The choking had left her voice hoarse. "Oh, lovely. Now I sound like James Earl Jones."

He threw his head back and laughed heartily at that, and she found herself mesmerized by both the sound and the sight of it. He laughed as if he had never once in this lifetime ever worried about what anyone else thought of him—with a full-throated joy and abandon that Bri despaired of ever feeling, at least in regards to the situation in which she currently found herself.

"Well, you don't look like him, so we're good," he said with a grin.

"You wouldn't do James Earl Jones?"

"No, men aren't my deal. I had enough opportunities for that when I was in public school. Not that there's anything wrong with it."

Bri smiled at what she assumed was his unintentional Seinfeld reference. "I know. I just love his voice. He wouldn't even have to touch me to get me off—he could just talk to me from across the room." She actually shivered, and he knew that she hadn't even realized she'd done it.

But he certainly had.

"I'm very," she pronounced the word very carefully, "aural." Bri immediately went to explain, "That means— "

"I know what it means, Jenny," he informed her smoothly.

She colored prettily. "Of course, you do. You probably have a much better education than I do, being British."

"Is that a matter of concern to you?" he asked, moving to sit on the couch, opposite her.

"Well, it's going to make me sound like a prig, but yes. I like smart people. That was one of the things that I really liked about your profile on the site—no grammatical or spelling errors. I mean, there's a spellchecker built into the site, for fuck's sake—use it!"

He gave her a small smile. "Well, I'm glad you saw something that caught your eye about me."

"That, and you're intimidatingly gorgeous."

"Intimidatingly?" he repeated, with a question in his voice.

"Oh, yes. I mean, when I responded to your ad, I did it on a complete whim. I really never expected to hear back from you."

Dom frowned. "Why not?"

She could feel that her face was bright red. "C'mon. You're gorgeous and I'm... not. You must have zillions of women on that app who are willing to pay big bucks to be with you." It had amazed her just how affordable his hourly rate was, too. That was another reason why she had chosen him, not that she was going to tell him that. "Do you mind if I ask how many clients you've had—or have?"

"Several." His answer was maddeningly vague. Several just now? Several over the time he'd been in that particular profession, if that was what it should be called? Bri really wanted to get him talking about what he did for a living, but she could sense that he didn't want to, so she let it go.

"Is Dom your real name?"

"No. It's what I am, and I think it's easier for people to remember, just because of that." His eyes narrowed on her, and she tensed, surprised to find that she had relaxed almost completely until then. "And Jennifer had better not be your real name, either."

"No, it's not. I've done everything the Innerwebs says I should do to make sure I'm safe." The fact that—before they'd met—he'd been very insistent that she do all of those things in regards to her own safety had made her feel that much better about seeing him.

Her phone began to chime a reminder for her to text a friend—well, more of an acquaintance, because none of her friends had any idea that she was there. "Speaking of which," she said, sending a quick text that she was fine.

"Very good."

It was impossible for her not to feel a certain sense of accomplishment at that bit of praise. She was still that same people pleaser she'd always been, at heart, although nowadays, since she'd moved into management, she had to do less of that.

"Are you feeling better? More relaxed?"

"Yes, I am."

"Next time, don't try to drink it all at once."

"You said a healthy swallow!" She leaned forward to argue automatically, then shrank back, as if she expected him to grab her and begin whaling on her when she'd done that.

Bran really didn't like the slightly terrified look she was wearing, although he completely understood it, and he also understood that pointing it out to her would only make her just that much more uncomfortable. So, instead, he leaned back on the couch, perched an ankle on his knee and said, purely experimentally—because he knew exactly what she was going to say—"Do you want to come sit on the couch with me?"

He immediately began to wave his hand in front of himself when he literally watched her tense back up again. "I retract that. I know you don't want to. Don't worry about it. In fact, I know you won't be able to do this, but you don't have to worry about anything—that's one of the best things about being a sub. You really don't have to worry about anything. That's what I'm for."

Her nervous giggle was surprisingly endearing. "Oh yeah. I am so not interested in having to be responsible for everything that happens in a scene. Way too much responsibility. Just the thought of that is enough to give me hives."

He grinned at her. "So what do you do in real life?"

"I'm in… well, let's just say the financial area and leave it at that." She worked for a bank, but he didn't need to know about that detail.

"Really?" He sounded surprised.

"Yeah. Why?"

Bran shrugged. "I don't know. We haven't talked that much, but I just got the feeling that you were the artistic type."

"No, I'm the 'nose to the grindstone', 'live for my work' kind, I hate to say. I've been working in the same place since I graduated from college. I've never once been late, and I've never taken a sick day."

"I know the type," he said, frowning again. "Never?"

Bri shook her head. "Never. I don't get sick much, and frankly, beyond work and a few friends—as pathetic as it sounds to me now that I'm saying it out loud—I don't have much of a life. I'm depressingly practical and predictable. I save my money, pay my bills, and go on the occasional trip." She fiddled with her fingers in her lap as he watched her intently. "I'll be staring all too closely at fifty in the next few years, and this is the most unconventional, unusual thing I've ever done in my life." She gave a self-deprecating snort. "And I began to regret it… uh… as soon as I booked you."

It was quite an admission, one she made while staring into his eyes, as if challenging him to say something critical or hurtful to her.

"I don't think you're at all alone in that. I imagine the times I've been stood up have been for exactly that reason."

Her eyes widened. "I can't imagine standing you up."

His soft laugh helped her relax more than the booze had.

"Well, thank you very much for that." Bri adjusted herself in the chair. "I'm not a very social sort. I haven't dated anyone since high school—believe it or not— and even then, it wasn't particularly physical." She shrugged. "I feel like I've missed out on a lot of life, and I've long since stopped waiting for Prince Charming anymore—not that I ever really was in the first place. So I decided that I'd do something I've always wanted to try."

"When did you know that you were into D/s?"

"Very early on. Like, earlier than it should have been, which is a red flag, from what I understand. But if there was any sexual abuse in my background, I don't remember it, and I intend to leave it that way. I've been reading D/s fiction practically since I learned how to read. It's kind of weird that I'm submissive, because I'm such a dedicated type A in everything else about my life. But maybe that's why—so that I can relax and let someone else take care of me for a little while."

Bran nodded. "I think that's a big part of it for a lot of people."

"Have you always been… dommish?"

"Pretty much. Like you, I'm a type A—although less of one now— but mine carried over into the bedroom. I very much enjoy being in charge there, too." He could see that she was breathing evenly and had vacated her ugly shoes in favor of curling her feet beneath herself. "Why don't you come sit on the couch with me, Jenny. You don't have to sit next to me, but I would like to be closer to you while we talk."

They had talked a bit online about what she expected

from their meeting, and she had told him that she was likely to be tremendously nervous and might not even be able to get near him at first. He had reassured her that they could take as long as she needed to, to feel comfortable. He had told her that he was a very patient man and that he wouldn't demand anything from her that she wasn't comfortable with.

One thing he'd said to her when they were chatting online really stuck with her. "This is not meant to be a race. It's meant to be a leisurely stroll. Thus, as the sub, everything will be done on your timeline, not mine, although I will encourage you to expand your comfort zone a bit."

It wasn't a demand, or even an order. It was more of a simple expectation that she would obey him.

And he was right. For all of her being an extremely motivated person who might have been judged by others to be somewhat stodgy and unyielding because of it, Bran could tell that she still had that "eager to please" component to her personality, too. Part of what he loved about doing this kind of thing was coaxing women out of their comfortable shell and introducing them to a place where they could feel safe without it and realize a more complete version of their sexual selves.

It took her a couple of minutes, during which he asked very neutral, mundane things, like whether or not she liked her job and how much of a commute she had.

At first, she had bridled at what he'd said. Bri hated to be told what to do. Then she nearly laughed out loud, considering she was paying him an exorbitant amount to do just that for her. Then, she took a deep breath, expelled every bit of it, and crossed the Rubicon to wedge herself into the other corner of the couch, as far away from him as she could get and still be on the couch with him.

At the same time, he rose to check out the honor bar again, turning with another pony bottle of whiskey in his big hand. He'd taken a stride towards her with it held out to her, but then he stopped, retracting his hand.

"When was the last time you ate something?"

"This morning. I was much too anxious about meeting you to eat anything after that."

He turned to grab another glass and poured the contents into it for himself before settling down on the couch again, half facing her.

"If I recall correctly..." and he did. He had a bit of an eidetic memory, especially when it came to his clients' likes and dislikes. "...you said that you'd never dabbled in D/s with anyone else."

"That's right." Bri cleared her throat, feeling nervous again, although she was trying to tamp it down.

"So you've never been spanked?"

"Nope. Never."

"Not even by your parents?"

"No, I was a very spoiled—well, as much as a middle class kid can be—only child."

"Ah." He nodded, as Bri marveled at his full head of thick, wavy, black hair. "And you said that was really the extent of what you wanted, right?"

"Yeah, I'm not into the heavier aspects of things—whips and chains, etcetera."

"You want a softer Dom."

"I believe so, yes. Is that usually what women want from you?"

"Sometimes."

She was very curious, and he was annoyingly evasive about his other clientele. "You won't talk to me about anyone else you're involved with?"

"No, I won't," he stated flatly. "Would you like me to talk about you with them?"

Bri shrugged. "I don't really care if you do."

"Well, I would never assume that about anyone I see."

His response was just slightly stronger than the others, and she sensed that she had offended him with her questions. "I didn't mean to pry. I'm sorry."

One side of his mouth went up in a lopsided grin. "You'll know when you need to be sorry, Jenny, because you'll be crying over my lap, and your bottom will feel like it's on fire."

He said it so casually, not even looking at her as he took a swallow of the whiskey. Her eyes widened at that, mouth hanging open in a surprised "O", and he just sat there grinning.

"I'm assuming you don't have any children?"

"None."

"No boyfriend? Lover? Fuck buddy?" He already knew enough about her that he would have been very surprised if she'd said that she did have a fuck buddy, but he'd encountered stranger things in this line of work than that.

"None since high school."

"Really?"

"Yeah."

"Don't you get lonely?"

She shook her head. "No, I really don't. I'm very happy with my own company, and I have a reasonable group of friends—seven or so of them—most of whom are women who are very much like me—they've only ever been single or had a short starter marriage early on, no kids, independent to a fault, dedicated to our careers, not dating now and haven't been for literally decades. We get together pretty frequently, and we all have the money—and the lack of commitment to anyone but ourselves and our immediate family—such that we can travel together at a moment's notice, go out to dinner or drinking and paint the town, not worrying about how the hubby is going to feel about it, or if the kids are okay." Bri pulled her feet onto the couch to sit tailor fashioned. "It has its advantages and disadvantages, like any choice in life. But for me, and most of my friends, there are more advantages than disadvantages."

"That's very interesting and very unusual."

"Yeah, I know. Out of my seven female close friends, only two of them have had kids. We always joke that—when we retire— we should buy an apartment building and move into it together, all of us single women, then hire a property management company to do all of the maintenance, inside and out. We'd have it made."

Bran nodded almost absently, a finger at his lips. Then he put his hand out between them suddenly, saying softly, "I want you to take my hand."

She regarded it as if it were a water moccasin, but he didn't retract it, even though he was pretty sure she wasn't going to do as he asked. His voice was just slightly stern, with a bit of expectation in it, too, but basically it was soft and deep. "You're a smart woman. You didn't go into this having not done as much research as you could about me and the service I work for. You've undoubtedly read the reviews left by my other clients, and you've checked out the company, too." Bran looked at her questioningly.

Her answer was quiet. "Yes."

"We are in a hotel room, and I guarantee that if you scream even once, the staff is going to come running. If you're as smart as I think you are, you already have the 9 and the 1 typed into the keypad of your phone. I'm bigger and stronger than you are by far, and if I had wanted to hurt you —rob you or worse—I would already have done that and gotten the hell out of here." He leaned a bit towards her, hand still out, words low and calm and comforting. "I am exactly as I have presented myself to you. I'm a Dom, and I very much like submissive women. Unlike a lot of Doms in my line of work—I don't shy away from women who don't have much—or any—experience. In fact, I like them very much." He paused for a second, then said, "I like you very much, Jenny."

She gave him an extremely dubious look at that, but he ignored it—for the moment. Bran could see that she desperately wanted to do as he asked. She was biting her lip hesitantly, but she was also leaning slowly towards him.

When her hand finally found his, he leaned slowly back, such that she had to move towards him in order to keep her hand in his—he wasn't holding it, and he didn't, even as she settled next to him on the middle cushion.

Well, it was progress.

Their hands lay between them on the couch.

"Jenny, are you a virgin?"

Her worried blue eyes found his. "You said we didn't have to have sex."

"And we don't. I was just wondering. You don't have to tell me anything you don't want to."

"I lost my virginity to Sean McCartney in the eleventh grade."

He frowned. "I can't do the translation from the American educational system to English educational system. How old were you?"

"Seventeen."

Bran nodded. "And you haven't slept with anyone since then?"

"Nope."

"No women, either?"

"No."

"Not even with all of those women around you?" he pried slightly.

"We don't live together. And we don't talk about sex much, surprisingly."

"Because no one is having any," he commented astutely.

Although she hadn't thought of that, even though it was right in front of her, Bri nodded. "That might well be the cause."

"Do you masturbate?"

"Yes, a lot less than I used to because I'm very busy, but yes, very occasionally."

"Good. I'm glad you do."

"You are?" That was a strange compliment, but she'd take it.

"Yes. It means you're more in touch with your sexuality than some of my clients are, and as we've discussed, all of these things we're going to explore are very much sex-adjacent."

Squirming unconsciously, Bri agreed, "Yeah, they are."

"I'm going to put my arm around you," he said, moving his hand out from under hers, to do exactly that, although he wasn't actually touching her, saying firmly, "I expect you to tell me if I do anything that you don't like or that frightens you, Jenny. Do you understand?"

Without thinking, responding purely to his tone, she answered, "Yes, Sir." Then she burst out laughing, covering her mouth to stifle the giggles. "Oh, I'm sorry. I'm just nervous and—except for being polite to someone who's held a door open for me or just filled up my gas tank—I've never called anyone that."

Bran was very glad to hear that she treated service people with courtesy. That was a characteristic that he had noticed was missing in a lot of people nowadays. He hugged her very gently with that one arm. "I know, and it's fine. If I recall correctly, that was something you wanted to do—to call your Dom 'Sir', and I think—as a rule— you should call me 'Sir' when we're together. "

"Yes, Sir," she whispered. It was so stupid, but Bri felt such a surge of satisfaction and pride—and arousal, if she was honest with herself—at the mere idea that she had been given her first ever rule.

She was stiff as a board, so he got her talking about herself and some of the places she'd been, which got her to the point where she was practically leaning against him as he moved himself a bit away from the corner of the couch, and he didn't even think that she knew that that was what she was doing.

While Jenny was still describing to him the experience of watching a wild seal pup being born in one of the bays close to where she lived, he gently guided her into place over his lap.

When she realized where she was, she tried to jump off him like a scalded cat, but he put his hand on the small of her back—no more, no less than that. He wasn't touching her with his hands anywhere else, and he wasn't even trying to restrain her with that hand. He wasn't exerting any pressure whatsoever—he just laid it there.

He didn't know why doing that worked, but it did—sometimes. Perhaps it was because it was only a slightly intimate place, perhaps it was just a reminder of what he could be for her—or that he wasn't making any demands of her whatsoever, but it was still something she imagined that a Dom would do—he didn't know.

If she truly balked, he would extract himself from her completely and move a bit away from her, so that they wouldn't be touching at all.

But she didn't. Instead, Bri found herself relaxing back down onto his lap, almost against her will, but she couldn't really claim that, because he wasn't really exerting his will over her in the least. He wasn't holding her there or in any way forcing her to be there. He merely had his hand on her back, and she felt very strongly—even on such short acquaintance—that if she had used her safe word or just moved out from under his hand, he would have left her very much alone.

Dom had been nothing but wonderfully caretaking and very courteous and caring with her since he'd gotten there. He must've thought she was crazy for being so hesitant and tense, but she couldn't help it, and he seemed to realize that, which went a long way towards her feeling better about being with him.

And when she lay down, gingerly, over his knees, he removed his hand. There was no instantaneous groping or grabbing or smacking away at her, either. He just sat there and she just lay there.

"Okay, Jenny?"

Bri nodded. "Y-yes."

"Good. Now, I usually spank a young lady on the bare, but since this is our first time, I'll let you off easy."

"You're going to spank me?" She stiffened.

Bri could hear the smile in his tone. "I'm a Dom. You're a sub. You're over my lap. Those weren't enough clues for a smart girl like you?" He frowned. "You do remember your safe word, don't you?"

That question struck fear in her heart, although she knew it was actually a very good question for him to ask.

"Yes, I do—It's 'safe word'. B-but I-I'm not sure I'm ready!"

"I respect that—although I would have bet that you were — and if you want to get up, you certainly can, Miss Jenny. But we're coming to the end of our session, and I just wanted to give you a taste of what it's like to be spanked by me, so that you can decide whether or not this is something you're really into or if it's something you want to remain a fantasy. It'll help you decide whether or not you might like to book me again." Impulsively, Bran said, "I'm going to put my hand on your back, Jenny. I expect you to let me know if you don't want me to do that."

It was the gentlest of touches as he began to rub her back slowly and comfortingly, like one would rub the back of a sick child. "I don't mean to make you feel rushed, though, Jenny. As I've said before, we'll take as long as you need for you to feel comfortable with me disciplining you. And if I've misjudged your readiness, then I'm sorry."

She'd never been massaged before—not since she was that sick child. But then, being touched by people she didn't know wasn't very high on her list of things to do. But it felt absolutely fabulous—much more so than she thought it should, to a disconcerting extent.

It did impress her that he had said that he was sorry, too. Non-dominant men had a hard time saying that, so it was very reassuring that he hadn't hesitated in the least to apologize to her—his potential sub.

Bri had to push herself to answer him, but she still sounded more languid and breathy than she ever had before in her life as his knowing hands turned her muscles— and her bones, it seemed—into jelly. "Well, that's not my only consideration. I can't afford too many sessions."

She'd set a cap of how much she wanted to spend on what she still thought of as a misguided misadventure, and she really didn't want to—or intend to—go over that. Even at his very reasonable rate, though, she wouldn't be able to see him too many times.

Bran hated that that was a consideration, but it was for some of the women he saw, which was why he didn't charge as much as he knew others did. He wasn't in it for the money; he was in it to help as many women have what he knew could be a life changing experience as he possibly could.

Although he wasn't much given to whimsy, he sometimes

thought of himself as something of a D/s Fairy Godfather, sprinkling what was almost always very positive, helpful D/s experiences to women who were curious about it. Some of them, he knew, had been satisfied and interested enough to graduate from him to full-fledged BDSM relationships. And some women—a relatively small percentage, he believed— he never saw again after the first meeting.

He really didn't want Jenny to be one of those, for a reason he couldn't quite put his finger on.

"I understand. As we've discussed, it's your decision. Our interactions will have to walk the line between delving into our particular interests—in which, if we were to fully immerse ourselves in them, would mean that I would be making decisions like this for you, based on what I know about you—and allowing reality to rudely intrude on our situation, unfortunately."

He was already thinking that he might offer her a considerable discount, if and when she mentioned again that she would have a hard time paying to see him anymore, and he'd never thought about doing that for anyone else.

The massaging was slacking off, and all of a sudden, his hand was resting on her butt.

Bran heard her gasp and stiffen at that bold move, but she didn't try in any way to get off his lap, either.

Seconds later, he heard a very soft, very tentative, "Okay."

He leaned a bit closer to her. "Okay? To what are you saying okay? Ask me for exactly what you want, please, Jenny."

Dear God, how could she possibly do that? She wasn't at all sure that the words would even come out of her mouth! Could she really ask someone—especially him—to spank her? Mentally, she knew that it went against her best interests, but for one of the few times in her life, she wasn't thinking with her brain, but rather her genitals, who were all for it.

"S-Sir," she whispered, "would—would you please spank me?" By the end of the sentence, he could barely hear her.

Another time— assuming she wanted to see him again, and he intended to make certain that she would want to do that— he wouldn't allow her to get away with asking him that quietly and shyly, but this was her first time indulging in anything like this. Bran didn't think he'd ever had a client with as little sexual experience as she had. It was amazing to him that she was still here and that she'd pursued this interest to any extent at all beyond the safety of her laptop. He knew that that was a testament to just how intrigued she was about having him do this for her—to her.

"Very good, Jenny," he praised genuinely. Bran couldn't imagine how hard that must've been for her to say.

Then he raised his hand, paused mid-air for just a second or two, and brought it down sharply—but not too sharply— on her rear end.

Chapter 2

HE DIDN'T WANT to turn her off, but he wanted the first swat she ever experienced to leave her with a realistic expectation of what being spanked by him would be like. Of course, he'd be a bit easier on her this time than he might have been if they'd been seeing each other for a while, but he still wanted to make an impression on her. He didn't want her wondering, moments later, whether or not she'd actually been spanked.

That would be another fine line that he would have to tread, but he knew he was more than up to the task. As much as he tried not to be egotistical, he was also a realist. For some reason, he had been born with a certain set of skills—some more general, some very specific. And throughout his life, he had done his best to enhance and hone those skills, whether they were in the realm of his personal or professional life.

And this was—in all humility—one of the things he was quite good at.

Bran kept the rest of the spanking in the same vein, not varying the intensity of the smacks very much, just delivering about twenty-five or so crisp, somewhat sharp spanks that would leave her knowing that she'd been spanked, and perhaps even a little pink, if she bothered to look afterwards.

He felt the lack of being able to watch her cheeks turn that beautiful, warm shade under his hand as he disciplined her, and he very much hoped that she did look, either after he left the hotel room, or later, in her home, possibly in the bathroom after a shower or in her bedroom, just because she wanted to see. And he was surprised to realize just how stark his desire to watch her do that was, not only imagining how she would look when she did that—the expression on her face, how her hand would touch her bottom cheeks gently, and she'd move around to get the best angle—but wondering what doing that might lead her to do.

Perhaps she'd even think of him while she was doing it— whatever it was that she did—but probably not.

After that first swat, which wasn't all that bad but still took her breath away simply because it was the first, Bri kind of braced herself for much worse to come. But it didn't—not immediately, anyway. Because she was excruciatingly aware of what he was doing to her, she could sense that he was keeping his strength carefully coiled. As he'd said himself, he was a big guy, and if he wanted to, he could really hurt her.

But nothing about how he had acted so far, or even now, had given her that vibe in the least—quite the opposite, or she would never have remained over his lap or allowed him to do this.

He was very deliberate, delivering each smack separately, and—in the beginning—on a different place on her butt. But —as much as she would have argued the point—she apparently didn't have that big a one, or he had a very large hand, which she knew was true. So very soon, he was smacking spots that had already received his diligent attentions, and that was when she began to experience the tingle that every story or article she'd ever read mentioned in regards to how it felt to be spanked.

And she had read every one of those over and over.

And over and over again.

What they didn't mention—or spend enough time on—was just how intimate that position inherently was. She didn't know why she hadn't thought about that, in regards to herself or him, especially considering how sexual this activity was to her. But not only was she terribly aware of just how aroused she was—and how her body was letting her know in no uncertain terms that she was—but she could feel how hard he was beneath her as his erection grew insistently against her stomach.

Bri could feel the warmth of his well-muscled thighs beneath her, could smell his after shave even more acutely than before, and, of course, she could hear him talking to her throughout the spanking in that unbelievably sexy British accent, in a manner that was just firm enough to distract her —slightly—from the punishment she was receiving.

"Now, I don't want you to think that this is how you will be spanked every time. This is your first, and I'm not spanking you as hard or as long as I would if I'd, say, found out that you had driven or ridden anywhere without a seat-belt, or that you had lied to me about something. The intensity and duration of a punishment will be in direct correlation to your misbehavior, and this is just to give you an impression of how I spank."

Just as she was getting to the point where she was becoming truly uncomfortable for the first time, he stopped, but his hand remained to cover her bottom.

"There are those who believe that the spanking doesn't start until the tears do. I don't necessarily subscribe to that philosophy, because I don't like to make generalized statements like that. Some subs barely need a tap to be brought back into line—in fact, just me being disappointed in her and lecturing her about that is more than enough to make her feel thoroughly chastised in some cases. Much more than that in the way of a physical punishment and she would begin to feel abused, which is the very last thing I would ever want."

As he spoke, he began to administer individual smacks to the plumpest spot on her bottom—and not vary the location, or the strength with which they encountered her backside —at all.

She hadn't felt the need to make a lot of sounds during the first phase of the spanking, or to move about much, but now she was moaning and shifting in place with every painful whack.

That was when she felt it the most and hated it the most —but still wanted it the most.

Exactly how screwed up did that make her, she wondered to herself, in a rare moment of true self-doubt—until the next swat caused yet another moan to escape her mouth unbidden.

"And then I have had clients who truly wanted to be beaten. I don't generally become involved with anyone who is like that anymore, because I, too, lean towards wanting to be a soft rather than a hard Dom. I can definitely be as strict as you need me to be— perhaps even more than you want me to be, occasionally, but only after you feel totally safe with me. But I like to think that—in my weird way—I'm helping my clients feel better about themselves, and I didn't feel good about myself for being that harsh, even though it was what they wanted. It just wasn't me."

He stopped spanking at the same time he stopped talking. The next slap, had it fallen, would have been the one that got her crying, and Bri was just as happy that that didn't happen. She hated to cry in front of strangers. Hell, she hated to cry in front of people who had known her forever—in fact, she really didn't. If she needed to cry, she did so alone.

But she knew—especially now that her bottom was relatively sore—that it was inevitable that she was going to cry in front of him. And although she knew she'd always find it terribly uncomfortable to do so—it would probably, also, be extremely good for her to get all of the stuff out that she had long since learned to repress.

No one in her family—or even her close friends—had been the type to wallow in negative emotions or tolerate a lot of drama. It occurred to her, for the first time, that she had surrounded herself with friends who were much like her parents in that way.

Bran left his hand on her rear again, and he could feel a certain amount of heat radiating from it—just the right amount, he thought. He patted her bottom, then said, "Come here, honey."

Just like that, without a thought as to whether or not he had the strength to do it, she was expertly turned so that she was sitting on his lap, being held nice and tightly in his arms.

Honestly, it was the most blissful thing she had ever experienced in this lifetime.

Aftercare was another part of the whole discipline scene that she very much wanted to experience, and Bri was glad that he hadn't forgotten that part of it.

He leaned back on the couch with his arms around her, looking down at her intently. "Are you okay, Jenny?"

"Yes," she answered without really thinking about it. She was absolutely okay, though. She was better than okay. It was the first time she could remember feeling completely and utterly relaxed. She was just floating somewhere, too, and feeling absolutely no urge to stay on top of the situation, to try to control what was happening, which went against everything she thought and was. Bri was still incredibly amazed that any of this was actually happening to her.

It felt almost too good to be held like that, against the warmth and strength of his body. If there was one big thing that she was beginning to realize that she missed in her life, it was not having had a real, adult relationship with a man, instead of just a furtive teenage one that was unsatisfying at best.

More than she wanted sex—because vanilla sex had never really been her interest—she wanted to be held like this. The only thing that would be better than this was if the man holding her actually had feelings for her, but she knew better than to think—at this point in her life—that she was going to be able to have that, and certainly not from him.

So she'd take what she could get. Perhaps it would be worth forgoing the trip to Europe that she had been planning to go on with her friends this summer in order to be able to spend more time with Sir. It surprised—and worried, a little —her that she was thinking that this soon, and she forcibly reined in her thoughts.

This was not a romance. This was a man who was being paid to do these things for her, and there would never—could never—be anything more than that between them. All she needed was to fall in love with this guy. She could not do that.

She couldn't.

She wouldn't allow herself to. If she began to experience real feelings for him, she would cut it off immediately. Yeah. Of course, she would.

And he did all of the things she'd told him that she wanted him to—rocking her a little, running his hands over her arms and back, and brushing the hair away from her eyes. Those, too, were highly intimate things, but they somehow seemed right, coming from him.

His tone was husky and low as he rumbled, "You did very well, Jenny. I'm proud of you. You took your first spanking very well."

In fact, she'd been so wrapped up in what she was feeling during it, that—until the last, more concentrated swats— Bran had noticed that she hadn't once even so much as kicked up or tried to wiggle away. He knew that that was a sign of how she was drowning in all of the intense, unfamiliar sensations he had brought her, and that was what he'd hoped would happen for her.

Bran watched her blush beautifully at his praise, noting that her expression seemed to reflect how relaxed she was now, and he was very glad of it, for her sake.

"Thank you, Sir."

Eventually, he began to gently and carefully move her off his lap. "I'm going to put you down, because I want to talk to you before I have to leave."

Every instinct in her told her to glom onto him, not to let him put her even slightly away from him, and Bri had to literally tell herself not to reach for him as he did so, as the familiar tenseness returned to her body and mind. He didn't try to separate himself completely from her, though, as if he knew how important it still was to her to stay close to him, no matter how much she was trying to tell herself that it wasn't. Instead, she ended up against his side, with his arm around her.

"Comfy?" he asked, and she nodded. "Are you feeling all right?"

"Yes, thank you, Sir."

She was very courteous, but it was almost as if she was using that to keep him at bay. He could feel that her entire body had stiffened, and he wasn't sure why. Usually, he could read that kind of thing in a woman's face or her body language, but not with her.

"Bottom sore?"

"Some, but not much."

"Well, I shall have to try harder the next time, then, hmm?"

"You don't have to do that," she answered shyly.

"Do you have any questions for me, lovely Jenny?"

He could tell that that kind of praise made her uncomfortable—there was no doubt about that—not that he was going to let her discomfort stop him from complimenting her.

"Do you always spank over your lap?"

"Well, that depends on what my client wants and needs. I believe that you had mentioned that over a chair or the back or arm of a couch or the end of a bed—along with over my lap—were all okay with you, so we'll probably try each of those during the course of our time together." He gave her a mischievous smile. "I wouldn't want you to get bored with me."

Bri snorted. "I don't think there's much chance of that happening any time soon."

He nodded. "Yeah, it's pretty potent stuff, isn't it?"

"Oh yes," she breathed, nodding exaggeratedly.

Bran waited for her to pose more questions, but she didn't. "Nothing else?"

"No, not right now, but I'm like that. I need to mull things over, and then more questions will come to me."

He looked at her pointedly, "Ah, well, don't hesitate to ask them. In fact, assuming that you want to see me again, I want you to be in contact with me between now and the next time. Just use the app and drop me a line. It doesn't have to be War and Peace. Write me about any questions that pop into your pretty head, but also about anything I did that you would prefer I hadn't, or that you wish I'd done more of, so I can tailor our next meeting to your wants and needs as much as possible. I also want you to let me know if there's anything you do during the week that could be considered to be naughty." He caught her eyes. "I can't be with you all the time, so I have to rely on you to be honest with me about your behavior. I find that my subs know when they've done something that I would consider to be wrong, or even just not good for them, and confession is good for the soul." He winked. "But I would suggest that you be scrupulous when you consider your behavior and how I might feel about it, because you do not want to spill the beans weeks later about something I should have addressed earlier. Do you understand, Jennifer?"

"Yes, Sir," she replied sincerely.

He turned himself a bit, so that he was facing her more, asking, "May I have a hug?"

Bri didn't hesitate one iota to throw her arms around him and hug him tightly, whispering into his ear, "Thank you, Dom."

He hugged her tighter, saying, "You're welcome, Jenny." When he leaned away from her, he asked, "Was I right in assuming that you want to see me again?"

She hadn't even thought it to herself yet, but still, she answered him in an instant with no regrets whatsoever at having done so. "Yes, please."

"That's good, because I would like to see you again, too." He stood, then looked as if he had suddenly remembered something. "Oh, I don't want to put any pressure on you, but I would book your next appointment as soon as possible, because I'll be gone for two weeks, starting next Wednesday, and I can tell that you need a firm hand frequently applied to your naughty backside."

Her lower body clenched at both his words and how he said them, looking down at her..

She followed him to the door, and he leaned down and

kissed—not her lips—but her forehead, saying, "Behave," then winking at her. "Or don't. That's more fun."

"Bye, "Dom"," she said, deliberately accenting his fake name.

"Goodbye, "Jenny"," he replied, doing the same thing.

"You did what with whom?" Tina asked, using correct grammar because—as an English teacher—she was contractually obligated to do so, even while texting.

"Well, you're the only person I can tell this to, because you're the only person who knows what I'm interested in, and I have to tell someone or I feel like I'm going to explode."

Brielle had stayed in the hotel room for a bit after Dom had left it and her, not doing anything of any great import, but spending her time sitting on the couch, staring off into space while she mentally sifted through what had happened between them that afternoon.

And, really, all she got for her efforts was a headache, so she got up and straightened her telltale disheveled clothes—at least she thought they were telltale, although it was unlikely that anyone else would know the reason why they had become disheveled—before heading out of the room herself.

Of course, the nebulous "they" would think that she and Dom had had sex, but they'd be wrong. She hadn't hired him to have sex with her—that was a step too far when she'd booked him. She couldn't imagine having sex with someone like that, especially since she hadn't felt that need very often until recently.

But she'd been entirely unprepared for the fact that being spanked was at least as intimate—although perhaps her lack of experience in that area had made her more sensitive to things that were—as he'd so aptly put it—"sex-adjacent".

Despite her headache—which was likely the result of having been so tense for so long, as she'd both dreaded and eagerly anticipated their meeting—Bri mulled those thoughts over all the way home. Because she had checked out of the hotel, she was also considering the fact that not only was she paying him, but she was also paying for a hotel that was of a better quality than she usually stayed in, because she wasn't about to meet him at a Motel 6. The higher class surroundings had helped her feel at least a bit more comfortable about what she was doing—although very little could really have helped her do that, but at least they didn't hurt.

But the costs might—they would add up over time. Not to mention the fact that she'd also chosen a hotel that was quite a ways away from where she lived and worked—not wanting to run into anyone she knew in the lobby or on the street—so she had a bit of a drive home, which made gas a consideration, too.

When she was finally back home, she took her shoes off and put them neatly on the boot tray that doubled as a shoe tray before she practically ran to her bedroom to take off her clothes. She put them neatly away, of course, before she allowed herself to remove the long silk scarf that usually covered it to stand in front of the full length mirror that she'd always lamented was on one of the sections of the bi-fold doors to her big closet. She had varying degrees of success as she tried to see the condition of her own butt.

She needed a bigger mirror, but she didn't own one, since she'd never considered them to be friends of hers.

Still, there was no mistaking how distinctly rosy it was. She thought that she could see a faint imprint of his hand, but realistically, she was probably just imagining it. She'd been fully clothed, and he hadn't spanked her that hard.

When Bri got sick of twisting and turning to get a better view, and as she cursed her lack of forethought in not ordering something suitable from Amazon before meeting him, she got into a pair of prim panties, yoga pants, a loose t-shirt, and a pair of fluffy slippers.

In his desperate need to try to kill her, her middle-aged marmalade cat, Morris, wended his way between her feet as she walked into the kitchen. No matter how many times she explained to him that—if he succeeded in doing that—he was likely to die, too, because she lived alone, nothing could dissuade him from trying to achieve his goal. Indeed, she'd fallen several times because of him, although none of the falls had been serious—so far. Her worst fear—which should have been, you know, dying—was that she'd land on him during that fatal fall, and they'd die together. The thought was both terrifying and depressing.

Bri fed him in self-defense, hoping that she would be able to move around without the imminent threat of death by cat for a few minutes, at least.

Taking a cinnamon roll—that was literally the size of her head—out of the fridge, she hacked off a hunk of it—complete with the cream cheese frosting—carefully setting it in a bowl atop a couple of pats of butter. After nuking it for thirty seconds, the house began to smell comfortingly like cinnamon.

As she settled down in her favorite chair, with a cup of hot coffee and the sweet treat she really didn't need on one hand, but desperately needed on another, she stared at it for a moment, knowing that she shouldn't have been eating it. But she'd just endured a very stressful event in her life—however voluntary—and she felt she deserved some kind of reward for coming through it relatively intact.

And not dead. Despite her cat's devious intentions—and

the fact that today's adventure could have ended very badly for her— not dead was always good.

There was something very soothing about cinnamon and cream cheese and butter and warm roll all coming together in her mouth. Damn her mother for learning how to make the most luscious ones she'd ever had! She'd never really ever been able to find any that were quite as good as hers, although these were the closest. Hers weren't as big as the one that she was currently devouring only a part of, but they were infinitely better because they had been made with love.

Come to think of it, though, maybe her mother had been trying to kill her, too, but much more subtly than the cat.

When she was done, she put the bowl on the lamp table, picked up her phone, and texted the person she was closest to out of her group of friends—Tina Farrell.

"Well, I finally did it, after literally decades of wanting to and being too chicken to. I let someone spank me."

And her friend didn't disappoint. Her response was just as surprised as she expected her to be. There was probably little else she could do that would surprise her more besides pulling up stakes and moving to Alaska, or quitting her job, or some other such ridiculous thing she would never, ever do.

So Tina's thoroughly appalled, "You did what with whom?" question was very understandable.

"You heard me,"

"You didn't."

"I did."

"No, you didn't."

"LOL. Yes, I did."

"For real?"

Bri nodded her head at the screen as she typed. "For real."

Seconds later, the phone rang.

"Why are you calling me? I thought we were the generation who didn't do phone calls? You're lucky I didn't send you to voicemail."

"You wouldn't dare," Tina said confidently. "Now tell me everything."

Bri snorted. "Have you met me? Of course, I would!"

"Besides, I didn't want to have to text all of my inevitable zillion questions. And first of all, who are you and what have you done with my dependable, practical, unimaginative friend?"

"Wow. Thanks for the thoroughly insulting character analysis."

"You didn't know that you're a stodgy, predictable, over-achiever who plans when she's going to clean her oven?"

"Well, unlike you, I actually cook, and it needs to be cleaned regularly."

"Stop that. We're off the subject of you letting some strange man spank you! Tell me everything! When did you meet him? You never mentioned anything about meeting anyone!"

"I just met him today."

There was a long silence from the other end of the phone, and then an even more disbelieving, "To-day?"

"Yes."

"You just met your new boyfriend and you let him spank you, all in one day? I repeat my question—who are you and what have you done with Brielle?"

Ticked off by just how amazed Tina sounded to hear that, she didn't correct her misconception about Dom imme-diately. "Is that really so impossible to believe?"

"Please. Hell yes! I have known you for a lot more years than I'll admit to, and I know you well enough to say that that definitely wasn't what happened. You are constitution-ally incapable of meeting a guy and then having him spank you—or have sex with you, either, for that matter—in the same day. It's also damned near impossible for you to lie to me, so I want to know what you're conveniently not telling me."

Having someone know you as well as Tina knew her could sometimes be a pain in the ass. "Well, it is the truth. This is the first time I met him, and I let him spank me."

More silence. "What aren't you telling me about what's going on here, Brielle Daley?"

"You were the one who assumed that he was my boyfriend."

She only paused for a second at that bit of information before returning, "Because that was the only logical conclusion I could come to, although that's pretty far out in the realm of possibilities, too, considering how long it's been since either of us dated."

"Well, you're wrong. He's not my boyfriend."

"Uh-oh. I have a feeling that I'm not going to like where this is leading to, but go on."

Bri knew that her friend was dead right about that.

"The truth is that I've been feeling a... lack in my life. I've felt it all my life, in the background of my consciousness, but I've ignored it in favor of burying myself in my work, and I've done pretty well for myself, I think. But I think that coming up on fifty brought it roaring to the front of my mind."

Tina had been an English teacher as long as Bri had worked for the bank, and—although they were both doing well—they'd discussed before that they were each also feeling the boredom set in. But they'd never graduated to talking about ways one might alleviate that boredom.

"Fifty? You have literally years before you hit fifty—I know, because I have years before I hit fifty!"

She sighed. "I know, but still. It's looming in front of us."

"Which is still better than the alternative, I'll remind you."

"I'm not arguing about that. I'm just saying that I've been feeling like I'm… missing out on something these days, and I finally decided to do something about it."

"And what," she asked, with great trepidation, "was that?"

Bri took the plunge all at once. "I went to a website and downloaded an app that matches Doms and subs and vice versa, and I found a guy I really liked. Today, we met, and he spanked me, and I loved it!" she positively gushed.

There wasn't silence from the other end of the conversation this time. Instead, there was a question that was full of hurt feelings. "And you did all of that without telling me the slightest thing about it?" Before Bri could answer her, Tina asked, "Did you even have someone to call and check in on you while you were with this man you were paying to hurt you?"

Brielle sighed deeply. "I understand that you don't get why I need what I need, but stop shaming me about my own needs."

Tina sighed. "You're right. I'm sorry. But your needs could get you into serious trouble, and I worry about you."

"That's very sweet. Thank you. And I did have someone checking in on me if that helps."

"It doesn't, because it wasn't the woman who has been your best friend since grade school."

"No, she wasn't, because my best friend from grade school would have spent the entire time trying to talk me out of what was an extremely fulfilling afternoon," she explained testily. But she did recognize the hurt Tina was feeling. "Look, I very much appreciate that you would have worried about me. But you would have been doing so unnecessarily. I'm home, I'm fine—I'm better than fine! Even if I never see him again, I'm going to have a lifetime's worth of masturba-tory fodder from him, just based on our conversations before we met, plus what we talked about this afternoon, as well as the actual spanking and aftercare."

"Aftercare?"

"A Dom—a good Dom—holds and kind of loves on his sub after she's been spanked."

"Did you have sex with him?"

"No, I did not, Christina."

"Humph," was all her highly articulate friend said.

"Yeah, humph. And, for what it's worth, I didn't mean to hurt you by excluding you. I was having enough doubts myself about doing it, and I knew that if I told you prior to seeing him, you'd be able to talk me out of it."

"Damn straight I would!" Tina responded, not bothering to hide her exasperation. "Are you going to see him again?"

Bri put her feet on the edge of the footboard of her recliner, letting her acutely bent legs fall apart to an obscene degree. "I haven't decided, although I'm definitely leaning towards it. He's cheaper than others, but he's still pretty spendy, and I'm not sure how many times I can see him."

"Well, before you make that withdrawal from your 401K, or take a loan on your house to see this man, you call me."

"What do you think I am, an idiot?"

"I don't know what you are anymore! The Brielle I grew up with and have known for entirely too many years has never done anything quite this dangerous and foolhardy before!"

Not for the first time that day, Bri found herself close to tears, feeling hurt and angry. "Well, now I'm sorry that I told you about it at all and made you worry that I'm going to do something you know that I'm not going to do because of it. I should have just kept it to myself, but I thought you'd under-stand how... how powerful and important this is to me."

She heard Tina sigh. "No, no. I'm glad you did. I wish you had done so sooner, but thank you for confiding in me now. Please use me as your security person from now on."

"No being judgy," Bri warned.

"No being judgy," Tina agreed. "So what was he like?" she asked, in a way that let her friend know that the lectures were over.

"Oh my God, he's tall and broad and handsome and absolutely everything I could have wished for in a Dom."

"You'll have to fill me in on that, because I have no idea what the qualifications of a good one are."

They talked for several hours, then, even though it was a Friday night, and it was only about eleven, Bri headed for bed. She'd showered that morning—carefully shaving everything she owned, even though she hadn't intended to sleep with him. It was better to be safe than sorry. So she got into her nightgown, climbed into bed, and put a news channel on the TV to drone on as white noise in the background.

Once the lights were off and she was under the covers, she reached for the end table on her right and opened the drawer to take out a pump bottle of lube and her favorite vibrator, into which she had recently felt the need to put fresh batteries.

She might not have had sex with him—and she was perfectly happy that she hadn't— but that didn't mean that —parts of her, anyway—didn't want to. Bri had been replaying the entire two hours she'd spent with him in her mind since he'd left her there, and her body was in need of more than a little relief.

And she was glad to feel that familiar ache again, after many years of it being dormant, shoved aside in favor of getting that promotion or working long, exhausting hours on a special project that got her a lot of acclaim but that had left her libido withering away in a dusty corner of her mind.

But Dom—she couldn't help but wish he'd told her his real name, but she understood why he hadn't—had definitely brought it fully back to life. Even just seeing his picture on that site for the first time had felt like he had breathed life back into—not just her lady parts—but all of her. Even before they'd met, he had begun helping her reconnect with the desires she'd kept tucked away for much too long, only taking them out on such rare occasions that she really didn't have to fantasize much to bring herself off. She really wasn't indulging her interests, even then.

And the sight of him, standing there at the door, looking tall and broad and more than a bit intimidating, was like a potent jolt taken directly to her genitals—as well as her brain, apparently, considering that she'd stood there, staring at him like a lackwit.

But she was getting off track with the self-criticism she was prone to wallow in. Bri wrestled her mind back to the matter at hand.

Him.

Just bringing him to mind was more than enough to get her clit jumping beneath the big, pink head of the vibrator as she pressed it gently against that little nub, amazed to find how far along she already was.

Out of curiosity, she reached down to her own entrance to find her fingers immediately drenched, not that she was at all surprised to discover that. Her panties had been wet the entire time she was with him.

Then she forced herself to settle back and revel in the pursuit at hand, wanting to savor every moment she could remember—taking things as they happened and trying to remember every single detail that she could about him.

The look on his face was so warm and open and welcoming—and that voice! Why did it seem that everyone who was British—especially every man—had gone through RADA and come out with a professionally trained voice?

She hadn't even gotten anywhere close to the spanking part of her mental replay of the events and she recognized that she was very nearly there! Bri could feel that familiar tingling that she did her best to fight back. And what put her over the edge—long before she wanted to— wasn't at all what she expected it to be.

It wasn't quite his voice, nor was it the way he took care of her at first, when she was so tense and upset—although it certainly contributed. She'd never before considered behavior like that to be arousing, but it was more his attitude while doing it than the actual acts. He'd done it so matter of factly, without seeming in the least hesitant and definitely not annoyed, as if it were the most natural thing in the world for him to do. But she knew a lot of men who would have backed away from an upset woman as if they had encountered a ticking bomb. Dom was comforting and just slightly—and perfectly—dommish with her, and it was still so unexpected that he'd knelt before her like he had, as if she were the Domme and he the sub.

His dominance obviously didn't come from a place of weakness that would be threatened by anything as ridiculous as a position he sat in. Kneeling or standing or with her over his lap, there was never a question in her mind—the entire time that they were together—that he was the one who was in charge, and Bri found that unbearably sexy.

But the thing that actually got her off was the sight and sound of him laughing when she'd said she sounded like James Earl Jones. He was utterly unselfconscious about that, too, throwing his head back so that she could see the strong column of his neck, mouth open, his throaty chuckle igniting nerves she didn't know she had.

Those thoughts had her hips bucking wildly, loud, animal

sounds coming from her mouth, her breath coming in great gasps as she rode her vibrator to more orgasms than she'd had in the past decade, combined, leaving her lying limply on the bed. During her travail, she'd thrown off the covers, and now she was drenched in sweat, panting heavily, her palms gripping the fitted sheet as the vibrator lay—forgotten —between her legs.

And she reveled in every single second of it.

She needed another shower, but that was an easy matter. In no more than twenty minutes, she was back in her bed, fresh and in a clean nightgown as her body was still vibrantly alive from the orgasms she'd just given herself. Bri wondered if she'd have a hard time getting to sleep because of that. She'd forgotten that climaxes were the best, most natural sleep inducer ever invented, and seconds after she turned off her light, she was dead to the world.

Chapter 3

THE NEXT TIME, when he knocked on the door of the hotel room, she was much less hesitant to open the door to him, although she did still check the peephole before she did so.

"I'm glad I could hear you unlocking the locks on the door. You'd be surprised how many times I come to a woman's door in a hotel and find it propped open with a stiletto pump."

Well, she didn't own a stiletto pump, but she didn't say that to him. Apparently, plenty of his other women did, which only made her feel just as dowdy as she had the first time they'd met, only for a different reason.

"Since I've spent my life as a single woman, I am very security conscious. I checked the peephole, too."

"Very good! I'm glad to hear it. I wish all women were that careful and aware of their own security."

Bri headed into the room, sinking into the occasional chair, but this time, she didn't have a breakdown, although she was only a little less nervous than she had been before.

Bran closed and locked the door behind himself, then followed her to the sitting area, where he again tucked his briefcase next to the sofa and removed the suit coat of yet another gorgeous suit—a different one, she thought, from the one he'd worn the last time she saw him.

Apparently, being a D/s gigolo was a money making proposition.

He sat across from her again, his soft gaze settling on her face. "Jenny?"

It took her a long second to realize that he was talking to her. She really wasn't built for this undercover crap, and it was hard for her to remember her fake name. She raised her head to look at him. "Yes?" There was a beat before she remembered to add, "Sir?"

He chuckled at that and patted the cushion next to him.

Branson watched her come to him, knowing that she was still feeling tense about being here, although he sensed that it was a bit less than it had been. But he wanted her near him, and he didn't feel that he was being cruel or insensitive by expecting her to sit next to him. He didn't even pull her to him when she sat primly down on the middle cushion, rather than cuddling up next to him, like a lot of women would have.

"How was your week?"

There were rumors floating around that the bank she worked at was going to be bought by a much bigger one and merged into it. It was likely to lose its identity entirely, and since the entity that was absorbing them was so much bigger, that made it much more likely that there would be a lot of people let go. That rumor, of course, was what was causing nervous texts and emails to fly around Headquarters— where she worked—as well as the branches and satellite locations.

But she wasn't about to bore him with work crap. "Same old, same old. How about yours?"

Bran had to smile at her. Although the women he saw

were rarely the selfish, diffident kind, it was still relatively rare for them to ask after him.

"Oh, I'd have to agree with you. SSDD."

That made her smile, and it was worth recycling a stupid old saying if it made her happy.

"Still," he asked, turning a bit more towards her, "is there something you can think of that you might have forgotten to do for me?"

She frowned, and he knew that she was actually wracking her brain to try to find something. It was something people said they were doing, but he didn't think he'd actually ever seen anyone do it.

"No, I-I can't say that I can. But maybe if I think more on it—"

"Don't bother. Your puzzler is going to get sore if you keep thinking that hard. But there was something I asked you to do before I left last week if we were going to see each other again. And you decided to do that pretty quickly, so I expected you to obey me."

He expected that that would be more than hint enough, even if she hadn't been paying any attention to him at all, and he didn't think that she was that kind of sub. She was the type who would remember exactly what he'd said and be able to rattle it off back to him at a moment's notice.

Not unlike himself about her.

And she was definitely not the type who could blow off something in an effort to be spanked. She was too rules-oriented. Jenny liked to do things right, and she would do her best to meet any and all expectations he presented her with.

But he could see that she was growing more agitated at the idea that she had failed to do something he'd asked her to than she needed to, and he couldn't resist the urge to wrap his arms around her shoulders. "Jenny, honey, this isn't life or death," he whispered softly.

"Oh, dear, I'm sorry. I'm just—it's not like me to forget something like that, especially in this situation."

"I know. Before I left, I asked you to keep in contact with me—"

"That's it! I listened to what you said," she interrupted eagerly. "You asked for questions, suggestions, etcetera. I didn't have any, so I didn't contact you." She looked very pleased at having been proven right.

Except that she was wrong.

"Well, firstly, I don't like to be interrupted."

He'd said it as calmly as he could, with no hint of reproach, but he should have realized that she couldn't take it as anything but a huge fault.

"Oh my God, I'm so sorry! I did it without thinking!"

Bran put his hand over hers, not holding them, just lying there over them. "It's okay. It's just something I want you to be aware of in the future." She still looked stricken, but he decided that drawing attention to that fact might just make the situation worse, so he pressed on.

"I believe that the first part of what I said was that I wanted you to be in contact with me between then and the next time we got together—essentially at least once a week—and to just use the app and drop me a line. Then I said, because I know some people don't like writing much, that it didn't have to be War and Peace. From there, I listed several things you might write to me about—questions, suggestions, etcetera—in case you had a hard time coming up with something yourself."

Her eyes were wide, and she was still looking fairly panicked at that information. "But… but I thought… you didn't say," then she thought better of that, "I didn't think…"

He curled his fingers around hers to hold her hands in his. "Look at me, Jenny."

It took her longer than he wanted it to for her eyes to find his because she was so upset, but eventually, they did. "I want you to take a deep breath with me, honey." She was becoming much more stressed than she should about something so small, and he lost her eyes. "Honey," he said soothingly, "look at me." He waited for her to do as he asked before he continued, "And listen to the sound of my voice."

And when her gaze only remained on his for a matter of seconds, and she seemed to be becoming more and more anxious, he said sharply, in a tone that brooked no disobedience, "Jennifer! Look at me, and do not look away until I tell you that you may."

Her eyes became glued to his.

"Good. Remember how we talked last time about the fact that you don't have to worry about things? Well, I meant it. There is nothing that I am going to allow to transpire between the two of us that should cause you this much upset. Even when you misbehave, you'll only ever get a spanking. It'll never be anything more than that, honey. Then all is forgiven, and that's the end of it. In the grand scheme of your life, I am a mere, hopefully enjoyable blip who should, hopefully, reduce your stress, not induce it."

Jenny slumped a bit upon hearing that. "Oh, dear. You're right. I'm sorry."

But that was an even worse reaction, because he could see that now she was upset about being upset. At that point, Branson didn't think, he acted.

Without realizing that that was what was happening—because she was so wrapped around the axle about not having contacted him this week when she should have, and how horrible an impression she must've made on him, and then she was also concerned about being so concerned—Bri found herself over his lap for the second time.

Only this time, it was more perfunctory and less coddling —more of a "real" spanking.

Bran didn't want to leave her with a negative impression of how she could expect him to spank her—novice that she was. But he did want to jolt her out of what he recognized as a spiraling anxiety that he only knew one way of helping her with—by giving her something else to worry about.

And within a few minutes of the time that he began to bring his hand down—much more forcefully than he had before— on her beautifully shaped bottom, he knew that he had already gotten through to her. She wasn't paying attention to anything but the possibility that he might swat her again in the near future.

And he did.

It wasn't a long, drawn out spanking, and it was much more than he had intended to give her this early in the game, but he'd done what he felt he had to and he didn't regret it, because it had served its purpose. All in all, it wasn't very many smacks—twenty-five or so. But they were all individual, distinct, powerful slaps. And he had literally heard her turn from whimpering and moaning and the occasional, plaintive, "Please stop, Sir," to crying softly by about the fifteenth swat. He added the last ones just to make sure it took, and she wouldn't begin spinning out again the moment he stopped.

And she didn't. She hung over his legs, crying, although not particularly hard. But he already knew her well enough to realize that crying wasn't something that she succumbed to easily.

"There," he said, pulling her into his arms with incredible gentleness. "You got your spanking for not being in touch with me this week. That's it. All done, forgiven and forgotten."

"Not by me," she whispered wetly, squeegeeing her hand over her cheeks to rid them of her tears.

Bran found her eyes. "That's something we will have to

work on, Jenny. That's one of the best things about having a D/s relationship, according to about ninety percent of my subs—the absolution. Once you've been spanked for something, I have forgiven and forgotten it—and that has to mean that you do the same for yourself, too, or else it was all for naught. For me, that's what brings meaning to the punishments."

He was quiet then, because he wasn't quite sure of what to say to her. But he kept her in his arms, holding her until she had again relaxed against him.

"I only ever got one 'B' in my life, and I hyperventilated when it happened, to the point that I had to be taken to the hospital."

He stroked her hair. "I'm not surprised to hear that. Have you never misbehaved at all?"

"I did as a kid, but my parents were very indulgent, and they only ever talked to me about it—my behavior. Since I was so eager to please, that was essentially all they ever had to do. The older I got, the less acceptable I saw errors, although I made some—infrequently. I learned to cover my tracks well, until I became an adult, and I found that there was a lot of power in owning your errors."

To her surprise, he nodded his head in agreement at that. She wondered what job he had had where he'd learned the same thing, or perhaps even been the supervisor who was impressed by something like that.

"Well, as I said, forgiveness is a big part of this for most people. They want accountability they didn't have as children and don't have as adults. They want things to be unambiguous, like they almost never are in adult life. So part of what I do is to make certain that if you do 'x', then I am going to—consistently—make 'y' happen to you, and it's going to be unpleasant enough that you're not going to want to do 'x' again." He caught her chin in his hand. "As far as I'm concerned, when the spanking has ended, you are forgiven. It is my sincerest wish for you, if you don't come away with anything else from our time together, I hope you will have learned to forgive yourself, Jenny, because you deserve to be forgiven."

To her horror, she broke down at that moment, dissolving into tears that made the ones she'd shed while he was spanking her look like crocodile tears. And he simply held her through all of it, not trying to stop or stifle her, but just being there, holding her in his strong arms and letting her cry it out.

When she had calmed somewhat, she sat up on his lap very suddenly. "Oh my God, I'm so sorry. I'm such a ninny. I'm so sorry to have bawled all over you and your beautiful shirt."

"Stop." He deliberately used a voice that would make her take notice and draw her eyes to his. "I mean it. Stop. You don't need to apologize to me for crying. You're going to be doing a fair amount of it with me, and I am not one of those men who gets all awkward and remote when a woman cries. I'd be a pretty shitty Dom if I did."

He was rubbing her back, and all Bri wanted to do was to return to his arms and let him continue to do that for her. "And as for my shirt, it's old, as is the suit."

"Old? Both of the suits I've seen you wear are way nicer than the CEO of the company I work for wears!" *Not that that would be all that hard to do*, she thought to herself.

He colored a bit at that but didn't say anything else.

She was very close to being relaxed enough to lean against him again when a thought popped into her head and she got all tense again. "Oh my God, I must've gone over our allotted time. Do you need to go?"

Bri made as if to get off his lap, but he caught her wrist before she did and pulled her back down onto his lap. "No, it's not. But that's another thing you don't need to worry about, honey. I can tell time just as well as you can, and if I happen to go over, it's my fault, not yours, because it's something I—not you—am obligated to take care of."

"Yes, but I don't want to short you on the money you've earned by being with me."

He smiled down at her. "That's another thing you don't need to worry about."

"But—"

Bran put his index finger over his lips, and her mouth closed with a click.

"Good girl."

To her surprise, he stretched himself out on the couch, keeping her next to him, trapped by and against his big body.

"Are you okay like this, Jenny?'

She nodded, saying much too enthusiastically, "Oh, yes."

"I kind of wanted to talk to you a little about something. I know you're hesitant about this becoming a sexual relationship, and that is perfectly fine. But would you be interested in the idea of me giving you an orgasm?"

"Now?" She sounded downright alarmed at the prospect, and he couldn't help but chuckle.

"No, not necessarily now," Bran said, although he wouldn't have minded doing that for her at all, and it certainly would be easy for him to do in that position. "I've found that a lot of women like one during the course of aftercare. Being spanked excites the nerves in that entire area, and most women become aroused by being spanked. Do you think that you might be one of those?"

She answered automatically, "No—"

But he interrupted her with a stern warning. "Don't lie to me, Jennifer. That's the quickest way to find yourself back over my lap, and what you just got will seem like love pats in comparison."

"I might be," she stalled, "but I'm not sure."

"There's one way to find out," he suggested, rolling the two of them such that they were lying face to face on the couch, his hand landing on her hip, very close to the area in question.

"Dom!" she exclaimed, without thinking, correcting herself immediately, "Sir!"

He wasn't moving a muscle. "Are you afraid that I'm going to hurt you, Jenny?" he asked, gratified by her answer and her vehemence.

"No, I'm not."

"Then what concerns you about the idea of me checking to see if you're wet? Would you prefer if I check the front of my pants instead, to see if any of your juices dribbled onto me while you were being spanked a minute ago?"

"No!" Much louder and more strident.

"Answer my question, Jenny. What are you worried is going to happen if I touch you there?"

"I-I don't know," she whispered, "and that's the truth."

His arms tightened around her, but she sensed that he was trying to comfort her, not restrain her in any way.

"What about if I did it over your pants?" She'd worn dress pants with a nice blouse to see him this time. "Would that bother you just as much?"

"I-I'm not sure."

"Are you willing to try it?" he asked, warm, coffee-scented breath flowing down onto her as she was held full-length against him, that hand still curling around her hip, his fingers resting lightly on her backside. "I promise you that I'll be very careful not to hurt you."

"That's not really what I'm worried about," she admitted.

She hadn't given him an out and out "no" but he tried to

be very sensitive about these kinds of things, and he didn't want to push her. But Bran did find himself extremely curious about whether or not she had been aroused by the spanking she had received.

"Well, I don't want to do anything that makes you truly uncomfortable in any sense, other than making your bottom sting."

Bran made as if to get up, but she surprised him by grabbing his shoulder to hold him in place.

For whatever reason, Bri was very uncomfortable about the idea of him touching her there, which was somewhat irrational, she knew. But she had decided to spend a lot of money to have his company, in hopes of trying new things.

And here she was, not allowing him to do something new to her.

"All right."

He gave her a doubtful look from under drawn brows. "Are you sure?"

Bri nodded. "Yes."

Her body was terribly tense and stiff as he began to move his hand towards her secrets, and almost immediately, she whispered, "I know now why I didn't want you to do it." He was surprised that she hadn't combined that confession by trying to stop him, but she hadn't, although he kept his hand where it was.

"Why?"

On a sigh, she answered, "Because I'm so out of shape."

His impulse was to chuckle at that, but he stifled it ruthlessly. The last thing she needed was him laughing at what was a huge insecurity of hers.

"Do you think that all of my other clients are skinny?"

Her eyes were downcast when she spoke. "Well, I doubt they're forty pounds overweight. They probably all look like Kim Kardashian."

"All of Kim Kardashian's weight is in her butt," he observed, in a tone that didn't sound as if he was much of a fan. "No one who hasn't had a buttload—*snicker*—of plastic surgery looks like that. And my clients are all real women. Some skinny, some not so, some very not so."

"Really?"

Bran smiled. "Really." He began to move his hand again, and she didn't stop him. Watching her very closely for any sign that she was getting upset, he let out the breath he hadn't been aware that he was holding as soon as his fingers found her and the evidence he was seeking.

In fact, he groaned softly and closed his eyes as his fingers dampened.

"Oh, yes, you are definitely one of those very special women," he whispered, before removing his hand.

It was on the tip of her tongue to ask him to do what she'd declined his offer to do for her, but she caught herself. She was trying to be more adventurous, but she wasn't ready for that step quite yet.

"Okay?" he asked, searching her face.

"Yes, I am. Thank you for asking."

"Of course."

"I-I like that you ask me that a lot. It makes me feel cared for."

"Good. That's exactly what I wanted you to feel." His voice became serious. "And you are cared for, Jenny."

She blushed at that, and he laughed softly.

"Well, especially considering what we both just learned, I want you to think about the possibility of me doing that for you the next time we're together. Why don't you write me this week and tell me what you're feeling about it. You could throw in how you feel about having sex with me, too, if you want to." He stood, then helped her sit up before he reached for his suit jacket.

Bri got up and helped him get his arm into his sleeve, although she had to stand on her tiptoes to do so.

"Thank you, Jenny. You're very helpful."

She positively beamed at that, and Bran had to wonder why more men didn't realize that a simple, genuine compliment like that every once in a while—that didn't cost him anything to give her—would have most women eating out of their hands.

"Thank you."

She followed him to the door, and he smacked his own forehead. "I forgot. I'm going to be gone for two weeks, starting next Tuesday. I don't know what my schedule—or yours— looks like between now and then," he said, using the British pronunciation for the word "schedule", "but if you can't find a spot before I leave, then, obviously, book one afterwards."

"Yes, Sir."

Again, he bent down and kissed her forehead, saying, "Goodbye, 'Jenny'."

And she answered readily with, "Good bye, 'Dom'."

Chapter 4

SHE STARTED the message to him at least twenty times—
and that was no exaggeration—typing diligently away at it,
then highlighting the text and deleting it with one keystroke.
Nothing sounded right to her. It was too trite, it was too
wordy, it was too unbelievably stupid and vapid and, and,
and. Of course, she had longer to get this to him than she
might have, since he was going to be gone for half a month.

It was then that a fortuitous message appeared in
her box.

"Greetings, 'Jenny'! I hope this finds you well! I was
hurrying out the door—which I hate to do—but still, and I'm
sorry that I barely remembered to tell you that I was going to
be gone. In future, I'll try to give you more warning about
things like that.

However, I'm writing to you to inform you what you
might not know, my being gone doesn't relieve you of the
need to contact me at least once a week."

Son of a bitch, she breathed. How did he know that she
was struggling mightily to do just that?

"And I want to remind you of something else, too. That

it *does not* have to be perfect! I am not an English teacher, although several people have told me that I look like I could be one, especially with the addition of wire-rimmed spectacles. And, full disclosure, I have played one, on occasion, to everyone's mutual benefit, I might add... ahem. Still, I promise not to return your missive to me full of red correction marks, no matter how atrocious the grammar or spelling —not that I think you wouldn't write well. I'd be willing to bet that you're one of those who takes a long time to send anything because you want it to be just right. I have wondered how long it took you to fill out your profile on the site, being the perfectionist that I know you are.

Anyway, back to the grindstone for me. I just wanted to make sure that I had made my expectations clear to you. Have a wonderful few weeks!"

Damn. Now she didn't have any excuse not to send him just one, but probably three emails, by the time she saw him again!

They'd last gotten together on a Thursday afternoon, so she carefully calculated that she owed him one no later than the next Wednesday.

And, as was not at all like her, but she found herself sitting with her laptop on her lap Wednesday evening, and absolutely nothing came to her. She never procrastinated like that—she got things done the moment she knew that she needed to do them—or as close to then as was humanly possible.

Why was a simple message so hard for her to write?

Stream of consciousness was something she'd never done —she was much too much of a planned person for that—but she figured what the hell. It would delete just as easily as everything else she'd written to him would.

"Sir:

In your message, you made 'perfectionist' sound like a

four letter word. And how did you know that I was sitting down at exactly that moment, trying to write something to you? Well, I failed miserably, and I'm failing miserably again at this very moment.

Having to write you a message every week is cruel and unusual punishment.

I'm long past wanting something perfect—having written War and Peace several times and deleted every word of it— and would settle for something that doesn't make me sound like a toothless Okie.

You asked me to address why I'm hesitant about letting you bring me off—before, after, and/or during a spanking.

The spanking—aside from the fact that I do find it excru- ciatingly arousing—doesn't have much to do with it. If you were a plain, vanilla-flavored... escort... I'd feel the same way about it. I've been so private, I've kept myself so scrupu- lously to myself for so long that I'm not at all sure that I could trust anyone else to see me that way—rendered all discombobulated and out of control by being swept away on an orgasmic tidal wave. And certainly never naked—more for your protection than mine (you've heard of Medusa?). So that kind of lets full-on sex out, too.

So, there it is. This week's epistle. Aren't you sorry you asked?

Great. Now I have no idea what to write about for next week. Sigh.

Jenny"

To her surprise, when she signed on the next night, there was a reply.

"My dear Jenny,

I didn't mean for it to sound like a four letter word. Some amount of perfectionism is a good thing. But too much of it —and I'm looking at you— is not a good thing.

And no, I'm not at all sorry I asked, minx.

Also, you have absolutely no idea what 'cruel and unusual punishment' *is*."

There was obviously much more to that sentence, but she wasn't at all sure she wanted to know what it was.

"I didn't know you were sitting down at that exact moment, but I can tell you that I would much rather have read all of your deleted writings—no matter how imperfect — than anything by Tolstoy, you toothless Okie. (jk, in case you don't realize that already).

As expected, your message was wonderful.

And, while I am aware of how private you have been and are currently, and as I told you even before we met, I generally spank a woman on her bare bottom. It's such a short, wonderful trip from there to your garden of delights (I have been known to indulge in purple prose, myself, on occasion). I feel it would be a shame for you to miss out on what I have been assured by many people—both anecdotally and by experiencing it, albeit second hand—is a pretty amazing experience. I'm not trying to brag about my abilities, either. Apparently, it's something to do with the dichotomous nature of the two forms of stimulation. It causes quite a… conflagration, or so I've been told.

I can assure you that if you should decide to grant me the honor of indulging in such with you, I shall do everything I can to make certain that you enjoy it to the fullest.

As to the sex, I would like for you to expound further on your concerns regarding that in your next weekly message, to which I look forward to with great anticipation.

Your,

Sir"

He wasn't even there and she needed a cold shower!

Bri had absolutely no doubt that he could deliver on what he'd promised her if she decided to let him make her come. In her fantasies—which, thanks to him, had come roaring back as if she were an insatiable teenager again—he had already long since done it, although that was no way to make a decision about whether or not she should let him do that to her in real life.

She thought about this almost to the exclusion of everything else in her personal life. At least he hadn't begun intruding on her work life. There, she would have to draw the line.

And, of course, it was Wednesday night again, and she hadn't sent him anything. She really had to get a handle on this shit! She did not like to feel so pressured to perform. It played hell with her anxiety—and her sanity, which was something she was coming to believe that she didn't possess all that much of.

"Sir,

Your last message had me tangled up in a ball to the point that here I am again, on a Wednesday night, with a message due to you tonight about a subject I haven't thought about once because of what you'd said about the other matter.

But what it boils down to is that I'm insecure about my looks, plain and simple (and that pretty much describes my looks). I'm frumpy and I'm overweight, and—at this late date — I'm not likely to change either of those things.

You, on the other hand, are drop dead gorgeous. You really should model suits for a living. You wear them perfectly, and you could probably make a lot more money than you do, as much as I would hate to lose you.

In that vein—the sexual one—you and I are oil and water. We don't mix. Maybe you should apply to become some rich old woman's boy toy. I can tell you that if I were her, I'd leave everything I owned to you if you'd just spend my declining years sitting out by my pool with your shirt off, speaking to me in that accent.

I would be much too horrified to ever be naked in front of you. Bare-bottomed, face down over your lap, I could probably learn to work with. But that's the bottom (snort!) line.

Please send me another topic to write about for next week, I'm begging you.

Jenny"

Again the next night, there was a message waiting for her from him.

"Miss Jenny,

I enjoyed your last message, even though the majority of it was balderdash."

Brielle frowned deeply at that line.

"I'm glad that you think you'll be able to be bare-bottomed with me, because that is how you will be spanked when we're next together."

She gasped out loud, fervently wishing that he hadn't told her that.

"I know you heard me mention that my clients are real people who look like exactly what they are—real people, who can't afford to get their teeth capped or their fat sucked or their nose straightened. No one is perfect, and despite your kind words about how you find me pleasant looking, neither am I."

"Pleasant looking?" she muttered with a snort. That was the understatement of the century!

"I gather from what little you've told me about your first and only sexual experience that it was not particularly enjoyable, and I would very much like to give you much better memories of what can be an incredibly wonderful encounter.

I happen to believe that you and I would mix amazingly well together—perhaps even explosively well, to our mutual benefit. Please think seriously about this possibility. I would very much like to replace that fumbling teenaged boy's no doubt insensitive way of relieving you of your virginity with an experienced, adult man's ability to provide you with a much more satisfying experience.

For your next writing assignment, I want you to tell me what you fantasize about when you masturbate, in excruciating detail."

"Oh, God, no!" she whined upon reading that line.

"Good girl for writing me, but I would suggest that you don't wait for the last moment. You never know when life is going to bite you in the butt.

Yours,

Sir"

And boy, was he right, since she found herself totally incapable of writing about the topic he'd given her to write about—her sexual fantasies, especially since he had become the star of all of them!

Bri arranged to take the afternoon off on the day she saw him again, but she very nearly lost that opportunity. Things were progressing much more quickly in regards to the merger than they usually did, and it was all hands on deck at the bank to make sure that every department was prepared to handle the effects of the merger. Most leave was being cancelled as a result, but her boss loved her, and since it wasn't very many hours—not like a three week vacation— she let her leave.

Bri would have preferred to see him on a Friday—just once she would like to have a weekend to digest what happened between them at a leisurely pace, instead of having to get up the next morning and head back into the fray like nothing earth-shattering had happened to her the day before.

And even what little had happened between them was very earth-shattering to her.

But his schedule said that he was unavailable on all Fridays and Mondays.

In fact, she'd peeked ahead in that schedule, just out of curiosity, and it had her wondering what it was that he did besides being a D/s escort. Aside from the two weeks he'd just been gone, there were several large chunks of time blocked out—for as far as his calendar showed, some of it relatively soon— during which he was not accepting book-ings at all, on top of the Friday and Monday restrictions.

That intrigued her to no end, although Bri knew that she had no right to ask him about his life outside of the time they spent together. Just because he occasionally offered her some generic information about his other clients didn't mean that he wanted to talk to her about his personal life.

When she let him into the room this time, he asked, "What time do you usually get here, Miss Jenny?"

"Why do you want to know?" she countered, noting that he was in another gorgeous suit.

"No real reason. I just assume, based on information already in evidence, that you're an early bird type, and I was wondering just how much of one. Like, have you just stayed here since the last time we were together?" he teased.

Bri laughed. "Like I could afford that! I got here at about two-thirty, or so."

Bran stood in the middle of the room, giving her a look. "Okay. But how early did you get here the first time we met?"

"Uh, I take the fifth." Then she asked impulsively, unable to stop herself, "Are you a lawyer in your real life?"

She saw him tense for the first time she could remember. That was usually what she did. "No, I'm not," he answered, and she believed him. "Besides," he said, coming to stand in front of her, "this is my real life. I'm real, you're real, this room is real. That's all the reality I need."

"I know, but—"

"No buts, Jenny." He brought her eyes to his and she'd never seen him look so serious, very nearly bordering on angry. "My private life—just like yours—will remain private. If you can't honor that, then I can no longer see you."

She moved a step away from him and put up her hands as if he were robbing her. "I'm sorry. I didn't mean to pry at all." She certainly didn't want him delving into her life outside of that room. "Your private life—and mine—is private."

His "thank you" was stiffer and more formal than he'd ever spoken to her before.

But then, it was as if she had never made him feel defensive at all as he caught one of her hands and tugged her towards him, until she was standing very close to him. "Someone didn't send me a message last week, even though I very generously gave her a topic to write about."

Her gut clenched. "I couldn't write about that, Sir. I just couldn't."

"Jenny," he intoned, sounding terribly disappointed in her. "And all you would have had to write was something akin to 'I'm having a very hard time writing about this subject. Would you excuse me from this week's assignment, please, Sir?' and I would have said yes as soon as I saw your message and we would have spoken today about why you found it so hard."

Bri grimaced. He might have talked about it, but she would have had a very hard time doing that, too.

"Instead," he continued, walking towards the door, where she noticed for the first time that he had tucked a straight-backed chair in the entryway, which he proceeded to pick up and bring back to sit in the most open area of the room, "due directly to your disobedience, I will be spending the beginning of our time together administering your first real spanking."

"My first real one?" she parroted back to him incredulously, as her heart sank, although it wasn't as if she hadn't known that her behavior was likely going to result in her being spanked. "B-but I've been spanked twice before."

Bran sat down on the chair, doffed his suit coat, which he threw over the back of the couch, and began quickly and efficiently—as if it were something that he had done many times before, and it likely was—rolling up the sleeves of his dress shirt.

And as much as she found the sight of him doing that to be alarmingly titillating, it also ratcheted up her anxiety quite a bit.

His eyes settled on hers as he continued with what he was doing. "How did I tell you that I was going to spank you today, Miss Jenny?"

Her, "Oh," was almost just mouthed, and the phrase that followed it wasn't much better. "On the bare."

"Exactly. And what does it say in my profile?"

"That you spank on the bare."

"Right again. So this will be your first real spanking, as far as I'm concerned. And, as I'm your Dom, and it is my responsibility to do what is best for you, it's my opinion that matters in this situation, Jennifer." Bran pointed to a spot between his knees, each of which was so far apart from the other that they were in different counties, and raised his eyebrow at her expectantly.

The thought that he could teach a class in manspreading flashed through her mind, but it wasn't the predominant thing she was thinking, which was how much she didn't want to obey him!

Apparently knowing that doing so would only add to her

problem, her traitorous feet automatically began moving her towards him, which was probably a good thing, although she wasn't at all sure that she could agree with that at the moment, especially since what she really wanted to do was to make a break for the door.

Not only did she not want to be bare from the waist down in front of this man, she also didn't want to be spanked by him on what would be her totally defenseless bottom! Still, she ended up standing right where he'd pointed.

She looked quite nervous, and he could see how rapidly she was breathing, but he wasn't of a mind to back down. Affectionate consistency was the best thing for Jenny, he knew. And a few nerves, especially in this case, where she was confronting several new things, which he knew was trepidatious for her, were to be expected. He was already hyper aware of her, and that would only increase, he knew, once she was over his lap, so he was relatively sure that he would be able to address anything unexpected that might occur.

Bran took her very cold hands into his and looked up at her. "Why are you about to be spanked, Miss Jenny?"

"B-because I didn't write you that last message," she whispered.

"That's right. And that wasn't because you just forgot to do it, was it?" he asked softly, still looking at her intently.

"No." She wondered errantly if forgetting would have gotten her spanked, too.

"No, you decided that you wouldn't do it."

Brielle felt as if she wanted to cry, and he had barely even touched her, but his firm, no-nonsense tone was more than enough to make her feel like that. "I couldn't!"

"Honey, I might not have known you for very long, but I already know that you're a very smart woman. And there's no way that you couldn't send me something—anything— even if it was just to say that you didn't think you could.

Some kind of attempt to obey in some fashion is always better than no attempt to obey whatsoever. Not trying at all makes me think that you don't respect me, or the authority over you that you've given me, Jennifer."

"That's not true!" Her statement was very strident, as if she very much wanted him to believe her.

But he was resolute. "That's how it seems to me. I enjoy reading your notes, and I was very much looking forward to this one in particular. But as far as I can tell, you just decided to blow off your assignment."

"I really wasn't trying to blow it of—"

"That's enough." His interruption was stern but not angry. "I know that you're very prim and proper, and I think it's good for you to explore your more... earthy feelings, by writing them down. But to send me nothing whatsoever is unacceptable, and what's more, I think you knew that it was, and that I would feel that way about it, too."

Bri hung her head. She'd never felt so thoroughly scolded in all her life.

He didn't wait very long before asking, "Do you want to take your pants and panties down, Jennifer, or do you want me to do it for you?"

Her answer was absolutely sincere. "I-I don't know!"

"I'll do it myself, then," he pronounced, tucking his fingers into the waistband of her dress pants so that he could undo the button.

Bri literally jumped at his touch, and he could feel that she was shaking with nerves.

His voice had changed timbre radically when he spoke again. It was much softer, without a trace of the sternness it had had previously. "This isn't going to hurt you, Jennifer. I'm just going to relieve you of what you're wearing below the waist."

As if she had no idea that that was what he was going to

do, she gasped as he brought her pants and underwear to her ankles in one efficient move. Bran bent over to catch them in his fingers as he put a hand out to help steady her. "You might as well step out of them; you'll kick them off while you're being spanked, anyway."

He heard her issue another sharply indrawn breath at what he'd said, but she did as he asked, and he folded both articles of her clothing—even her panties—very neatly, putting them over the back of the couch next to his coat.

Then he guided her to the right of his legs and helped her lie over them. One arm automatically reached across her back to keep her from falling off, although his thighs were more than long enough that there was much less danger of that with him than with a shorter man.

At first, he adjusted himself and her, then, with both arms resting on her, he said, "You have a very beautiful bottom."

Bri snorted. She did it without thinking. It was an automatic response to pretty much any compliment, honed by decades of self-derision about her looks.

"I'm sorry. What did you say?" he asked sharply, letting his palm cover her very vulnerable butt in warning. Bran felt her flinch when he did so.

"I didn't say anything," she replied, her voice barely above a whisper.

"Well then, you're going to need to learn to keep noises like that—the kind that make me think that you think I'm a liar—to yourself."

He paused, but she didn't say anything.

"Yes, Sir?" he prompted.

She arched up suddenly, as if he'd woken her up, but he knew that she was just preoccupied by the newness of the position in which she found herself, as well as what she knew was going to happen to her in the next few minutes. "Yes, Sir!"

"That's better."

And Bran was not lying—from his angle, she had a beautiful, delightfully generous backside, although he knew that she had faced a lifetime of being told that she wasn't attractive, something in which her mother might even have had a hand, although he hoped not.

"I'm going to spank you, Jennifer, and you can, and will, I promise you, cry and scream and moan and whimper, all you want, although you may not curse at me. You can—and will—kick your feet up and try to wiggle your way off my lap. I can deal with that. But if you reach back to try to prevent a swat from landing, I will keep possession of your hand until the spanking is over, and you will have earned yourself an extra twenty swats on what will be—and I promise this, too—a bottom that you do not want touched for any reason, much less for added smacks."

Bran rubbed her back for a moment. "Do you understand?"

"Yes," she whispered.

"Louder than that, honey."

"Yes, Sir."

"Very good."

She was able to remain quiet for the first ten or so—pretty much, anyway. The swats he was delivering were bad—being spanked on her naked behind was infinitely worse than having some—any—kind of barrier between herself and his palm. But at first, anyway, they weren't too horrendous. But as he spanked her—slowly and methodically and inexorably—the accumulated sting began to compound and rise to a truly terrible level.

Bri thought she would be able to take most spankings without too much of a fuss—maybe some yelps or cries or groans—but, boy, was she wrong! And she had absolutely no idea how many smacks he intended to give her! She was too nervous to have kept a count in her head, so she had no idea how many she'd received before they got to be very hard to take, and she couldn't keep a sound thought in her head.

If wasn't very long at all before she'd stopped worrying about being naked from the waist down and blatantly trying to throw herself around—unathletic though she was—kicking her feet, grabbing the leg of the chair, and at one point, his leg, and trying to twist herself in a manner she hadn't been able to when she was a kid, much less now.

But she still attempted it, however in vain. Bri would have done pretty much anything to get him to stop. More than once—hell, with every swat—she wanted to put her hand back there in hopes of preventing even just one from landing right where he intended it to.

She managed not to, but it was just by the skin of her teeth.

There was no telling how long it went on. Time didn't mean anything to her; the only thing that was real to her for those very long moments were those relentless, horrible, God-awful spanks, and the possibility of him stopping them, hopefully in the very near future.

At first, he didn't speak at all—she was the one making all of the noise. When it was just beginning to get to the unbearable point, he abandoned his silence, and she was very glad he did. It wasn't much help, but the sound of his voice was at least something that—at its core—was comforting to her, on a very basic level, whether or not he intended that it be, and somehow she doubted that he did.

"I know that it's hard for you to talk about things like what I asked you to explore, but just because it's hard, doesn't mean that you don't have to at least make some attempt to do it. I've said that I don't care what the writing is like. I've said that it doesn't have to be War and Peace. I just want to see something that tells me that you made some kind of effort to do as I asked, and I don't think that that's too much to expect from you when you have a week in which to do it, Jennifer. It was very naughty of you to simply not bother to do anything at all. That is an act not just of disobedience, but of disrespect, and I will not tolerate either of those things from you. I hope that I am making myself very clear about that, or the next time this happens, you'll get much worse than this for having been spanked before for the very same transgression."

Once he'd finished his chastising little speech, he went back to being quiet, and she felt the lack of even that small amount of succor very acutely.

Bri was so deeply attuned to her own misery that it barely registered to her when he finally stopped. He didn't try to move her in any way or make her get up. He remained in the same position, but his arm was no longer the strong presence keeping her in place that it had been. Instead, he was running both of his hands over her back comfortingly while she continued to weep—and drool—on the carpeting.

But she was well beyond caring about either of those things. And thus, she was thoroughly unprepared for what he said next.

His arm returned to its previous place, holding her less insistently than before, but then she wasn't a whirling dervish trying to avoid pain, at the moment, so it didn't need to be. Still, it was a good, firm hold.

"Jenny," he began. Apparently, the punishment had transformed her back to that. "I want to know if you're wet."

Chapter 5

DURING THE COURSE of the past few very long moments, all dignity and modesty had flown from her with the strict cadence of the slaps she was receiving. He'd called her "prim and proper", but that phrase didn't describe her as accurately at that moment. There was no telling what he'd seen of her while he'd been spanking her, and she had long since graduated beyond the point of caring.

She hung over his lap like the limp rag she felt she'd been reduced to.

"If I don't hear any objections, then I'm going to do that."

He paused for what was a very generous amount of time.

But she just couldn't summon the energy—or, frankly, the desire, although she knew she should want to—to try to prevent him from doing that, even in the most elemental way of just saying "no".

It surprised him that she didn't even make an attempt or voice any kind of objection, but he very much wanted to find out the answer to his question. He did so as quickly and efficiently as he could, as much as his fingers and hand wanted to linger at that spot between her legs, which, to his great gratification was sloppily wet.

On his way out, he couldn't resist slipping the pads of his very slippery index and middle fingers over her clit quite deliberately.

That drew a response from her—a guttural groan as she arched up, although he wasn't sure if it was in protest at what he'd done, or because him touching her like that was unexpected—or arousing.

Bran was well satisfied with his efforts, but instead of sitting there congratulating himself, he realized that she was probably becoming uncomfortable from the position she was in.

So, before she could say "yea" or "nay", he stood with her in his arms and walked over to the couch, where he arranged her on his lap again but held tightly in his arms. As soon as her head found his chest, she began to cry again, and he held her through it, adjusting her position slightly here and there, kissing her temple occasionally, handing her a tissue when there was a break in the storm. But really, he was just there for her, providing her a warm, comfortable, safe place for her to recover from what was undoubtedly an eye opening experience for her on a lot of different levels.

When she had quieted, and he thought she might have fallen asleep on him—which he would completely understand—he felt her shift against him. "Are you okay, Jenny?" he asked, and she thought she detected a bit of anxiousness in his tone.

"I'm fine," she answered quietly.

That didn't surprise him in the least. Many subs were quite subdued after they'd been punished.

"Would you like me to put some lotion on your bottom? I've been told that it can be very soothing, and I'll be very careful not to hurt you."

"Yes, please." She nodded.

He helped her back into the same position, but this time, she wasn't hanging down. She had the support of the couch —front and back—that the straight-backed chair hadn't provided.

Bran made a note that that might not be the best position in which to spank her.

She folded her arms beneath her head, turning it so that she was looking away from him. He leaned a bit forward to grab his briefcase, just long enough to take what he needed out of it and put it on the couch next to him.

The lotion that he used was cool and floral-scented, and as he spread it over her very sore looking red bottom, she groaned again, in a manner that had him coming to attention beneath her, although she didn't seem to notice.

"Poor baby," he crooned, and Brielle ate up every bit of his sympathy he was willing to offer her as his hand soothed the lotion over her angry behind. His tone nearly hypnotic, he whispered, "But it's all over now, Jenny, and you are completely forgiven. I want you to try to remember that for me."

"Yes, Sir," she said, but he knew that it was a rote response—that she didn't believe it, and she likely didn't forgive herself. "Thank you for doing this."

"You're very welcome, honey," he replied with a small smile that she couldn't see.

Bran took his time, making certain to cover every single inch of her inflamed flesh, and when he finished, he grabbed the handkerchief from his pants pocket and used it to wipe off his hand.

Then he took the pump bottle of lube—that he probably didn't even need to use with her, he realized—and was going to put a little onto his fingers, but he decided he was getting ahead of himself, and instead said, "Jenny, I want to touch you, honey. Let me give you a little pleasure to alleviate some of the discomfort."

She had turned her head quickly at his first sentence, although it was still resting on her arms, and she deliberately sought his eyes, as if she thought that that was where she could find the answer to whatever nebulous question she was thinking of at the moment.

She hadn't gotten up, she hadn't stiffened, and she hadn't told him no—yet.

But she also hadn't told him yes.

And Bri never really did. She wanted to, but she couldn't quite bring herself to do it. So, instead, she reached down to find his arm and follow it down to his hand, where she tucked her hand into his. Warm, strong fingers closed around it, and she turned her head back so that she was no longer looking at him.

Well, it wasn't an enthusiastic "yes", but he'd given her plenty of ways to tell him "no". He was going to chance it anyway, because it was very much what he wanted to do for her, and if he were honest with himself, he was doing it for his own benefit, too.

Now that the moment was at hand, Bran took a deep breath, consciously making certain that he didn't approach her with a timeline in mind. He didn't want her to feel rushed or pressured in any way. If they went over her time, he'd eat it and be damned happy to, especially if he was able to get her off, and he was pretty sure he could.

He didn't dive right into her most sensitive place, either. Instead, he ran his hand slowly over the backs of her legs, down to her feet and back, noticing that her toes were cold. He'd bring warm slippers for her next time. Then he used just the tips of his fingers and retraced his steps, although he avoided touching the bottoms of her feet, because he remembered that her profile had said that she was very ticklish and didn't enjoy being tickled at all.

But as soon as he'd brought his fingers up her far thigh, he didn't stop there. He dragged them—gently—over her extremely red backside, causing her to hiss in her breath. Bran did the same thing to her other cheek, and only then did he begin to address the heart of her.

"Open your legs a little for me, Jenny."

She obeyed him immediately. That was one of the perks of having a freshly spanked sub—they tended to be almost overly accommodating, at least until their butts stopped stinging.

"Good girl," he praised, hearing her whimper slightly. He wished that her face wasn't turned away from him, but he knew that it was probably easier for her that way. And, this first time, he wouldn't give her any rules. Truly, all he desired at the moment was to please her, so whatever she wanted was fine with him.

But there would come a time when he wouldn't allow her to hide all of the tiny, indrawn breaths, the barest of whimpers, or the revealing expressions that might give away a lot of how she was feeling, and he very much looked forward to learning about even the smallest of things that gave her pleasure.

Slowly, very slowly, he pressed his hand over the outside of her groove, until he could feel the top of her outer lips, having gotten his entire hand wet from her juices. Because she hadn't necessarily planned on letting him do this, he didn't have anything to go on about her likes and dislikes— she'd skipped that section of her profile. So he was having to wing it and extrapolate as best he could from what little he already knew about her, not that he thought that was going to be any kind of a problem for him.

As he brought his hand back down, he let his fingers part

her lips and glide over her clit, then down to the source of her honey. Knowing how inexperienced she was, it was just his index finger that he pressed experimentally against her opening, and it barely went in at all, barely even to his first knuckle. He didn't find any real resistance, but she was excitingly, incredibly tight.

His cock was just about ready to explode when he discovered that, and Bran had to ruthlessly force his own desires into the background in order to concentrate on hers in the way he wanted to.

It was a definite source of pride to him that she was as wet as she was, but her dew didn't have the viscosity of the lube he'd brought, so he squirted some on his fingers before returning them to their place between her legs. As much as he wanted to use his fingers to open her farther, that would be more a pursuit that pandered more to his desires than hers. At the moment, he didn't want to risk the possibility that she might not consider him entering her in any way to be a pleasant experience.

So he vowed to save that for another time and slathered that dollop of slickness right on top of her clit.

When he did that, Bri tensed quite a bit, squeezing his hand fit to break it.

"Relax, baby," he encouraged in a low, comforting tone. "I'm not going to let anything happen that doesn't feel absolutely amazing to you."

Bran wasn't sure whether it was what he said or what she was feeling, but she abandoned his hand entirely in favor of clenching her fist by her side, and he was surprised to feel the loss of it.

But it was the sheer depth of her groans that really got to him, and the way that she writhed beneath his hand. He could hear the breath hissing in between clenched teeth as he teased her relentlessly, feeling her swell and harden beneath the pads of his fingers. Bran deliberately used his other hand on her back to apply just the slightest pressure, to give her the barest hint of feeling restrained by him, held down by his superior strength so that he could do this to her, as her Dom.

And it worked for her, too—all too well! Suddenly, she was right there—pretty much on the verge, but for some weird reason, her mind seemed to want her to pull back from that edge, as if she was worried that he might think badly of her because she was so quick to come.

"That's right, honey." Some of the sounds she was making made him wonder if she was in pain, but her body kept reminding him that no, it was pleasure, as incontrovertible evidence of that fact bathed his hand continuously.

"Sir, Sir, Sir, Sir, Sir," she began to chant under her breath, as he expertly brought her closer and closer and closer, but she couldn't seem to actually get there.

"Yes, honey?"

"I-I, oh, my god! I can't, I can't, I can't!"

He stopped touching her immediately, although his hand remained there. "Why not, baby? Is something wrong?" Bran's body was tense, wondering if he was hurting her or she was sick or something worse than that.

There was no way she could explain her predicament to him. "No," she practically growled at him. "Something is unbearably right! But I-I can't. I c-can't take m-much more!"

Not knowing about the mental block she was experiencing, Bran was glad she couldn't see the self-satisfied grin that spread over his face. Since it had been so long for her, he had wondered if it might not take quite a while. She was full of surprises! "I'm very glad to hear that, honey. You may come any time you feel the need to, but I'm not going to stop until you do."

Bri hadn't thought that he might want to control her orgasms—that he might expect her to ask him for permission to come, which she found incredibly erotic. She'd also never thought about being forced to orgasm against her will, and that was at least as hot a concept as having to get permission to do so!

As he continued to flick that delicate pearl of hers, Bran leaned over so that she could hear him better, saying, "At some point, I'm going to put my mouth where my hand is, and I'm going to make you come until you beg me to stop."

"No!" she barely breathed.

"Oh, yes. I'm afraid so. You do realize that you no longer have control over your own orgasms?"

That was it. That was what did it—regardless of what her mind was telling her, that was all she could take.

On a very loud scream, while she literally humped his hand as it continued to worry her little bean, Bri came so hard that she very nearly lost consciousness. She did expel every bit of air from her lungs on that scream, then dragged it back in and let loose another one.

As much as he didn't want to, Bran leaned over and put his hand gently over her mouth.

She cut off the scream immediately, mortified at having done that at all, much less twice! She'd never done that in her life and was horrified at the possibility that she might have brought the cops—or hotel management—or anyone else in authority to their door. Bri's first instinct was to try to get up, but—in the first time he'd done that—Bran did use his superior strength to keep her right where she was.

"I didn't mean you had to stop," he said, continuing to stroke her while listening and watching her body trying to respond to his efforts, while he knew—now—that it was her overactive mind that was getting in her way. "Far from it. I just wanted to make you aware of the volume of your cries." The crooning quality of his voice changed, and the next thing he said was much sterner. "Lie back down, please."

He felt her body tense, but not in the way he wanted it to, and she remained like that for a few seconds before her intellect lost the battle and she collapsed down onto his lap again.

"Good girl," he said, and although she wasn't quite as abandoned as she'd been before, he recognized the signs of her second orgasm, tucking away the bit of information he'd learned about her with its very quick arrival—she was definitely a praise slut.

She didn't experience as many climaxes as he would have liked her to, but for a first time, it was pretty darned good— at least from his position, it seemed to be. Bran figured that she'd had five or six or so good, hard orgasms, and he looked forward to a time when he could restrain her and discover what her limit was.

The disturbing thought crept into his mind, though, that she might not be able to continue seeing him long enough for them to get to that point. In fact, someone else might be the one to do that to her—for her. And it could be someone who might not appreciate her as much as he did, who wouldn't take as good care of her as he did, either. The unknown stranger he'd conjured in his mind might actually not be at all good for her and might potentially hurt her, either immediately or down the road.

He shoved all of those worrying thoughts out of his head, though, in favor of gathering her against him. Bran turned so that they were stretched out and facing each other on the couch, so that he could give her a full body hug. She clung to him, and it felt unbelievably wonderful, because he was so well aware of the fact that she was not at all the clingy type—just the opposite, in fact. He took it as an incredible compliment that her arms were wrapped so tightly around him.

Hell, he took it as an incredible compliment that she was still in the room with him, that she'd been in a hotel room with him before, and that she'd had the courage to decide that she wanted to pursue her passion and had picked him in the first place, considering how he knew she'd run her life for the past he didn't know how many years—not that he cared.

He knew that his cock was fully erect and pressing insistently into her tummy, and—not for the first time—he wished that there was some kind of switch he could throw to get rid of an inconvenient erection. But there wasn't, so he just ignored it. He wasn't about to ruin a time that he had very deliberately crafted and created just for her with his own demands.

Still, Bran couldn't seem to keep his hands off her. He kept running them over her sides, or brushing back her hair, or rubbing her back, not that she seemed to mind in the least.

After a long while, Bri leaned away from him. "Oh, Sir, thank you so much for that." Tears were right behind her eyes as she said that to him, but she held them back. "I can't even tell you how— " She stopped, because she knew she couldn't go on without losing the battle to hold them at bay.

He well realized how hard it was for her to say anything like that to him. "You're very welcome, Jenny, honey. It was an incredible thing to watch, and I'm very honored that you let me do that for you. I know it was something you weren't sure about, and I hope I didn't pressure you too much into doing it."

She shook her head. "No. It was what I wanted, but sometimes, I can't seem to allow myself to do what I want."

He grinned. "I'll be only too glad to help you with that." Impulsively, he leaned down and kissed her once, very gently, making them both very aware that this was their first kiss.

Then, somewhat embarrassed that he'd done that—and he didn't get embarrassed about much of anything anymore —Bran forced himself to pull away from her and stand up, when all he really wanted to do was to spend the rest of the day and night indulging himself with her.

Bri sat up, feeling very discomfited as she put her hands over her mouth, saying, "This time I know I must've run over. Send me a message and let me know what I owe you."

"No way. Like I said, I'm the Dom, and it's my responsibility to keep track of my time—not yours."

"But, Sir, " she glanced down at her phone, "we're nearly an hour over! I want to pay you what I owe you, please."

Shrugging back into his suit coat, he gave her a look as she stood. "What did I just say, Jenny?"

She looked adorably worried about him, as if she thought he'd be destitute if she didn't pay him what she thought she owed him. "That you'd take care of it."

"And what did I mean when I said that, Jenny?" he asked, coming to pull her against him.

"That you'd take care of it," she answered, not looking at him. "But—"

His hand found her bottom and squeezed it just slightly, making her gasp and jump before he let go, moving away from her to grab his briefcase. "End of subject, Jennifer, unless you'd like me to use another hour teaching you another lesson?" he asked, looking back at her with his eyebrows raised.

Her own hands went to her backside, as if to protect it from that fate. "No, thank you. You're the master of your time, not me."

"Damn straight," he growled, then grinned at her like an idiot. As he headed for the door, Bran said, "You still owe me a message about your fantasies from last week, and that's on top of what you owe me this week, which I want to be about how you felt about what just happened between us—all of it."

Bran heard her groan at that pronouncement, sounding

as put upon as if he'd assigned her to perform some of the trials of Hercules.

He needed to get going, but he still took the time to pull her to him and give her a warm hug that didn't seem rushed in the least, kissing her forehead. "Goodbye, 'Jenny'."

"Goodbye, "Dom"."

Chapter 6

"SO, how is it going with your gigolo?" Tina asked as she came around the end of her car to meet Brielle. They were in a beautiful cemetery along a picturesque estuary in the small town south of Boston where they both lived. As they'd commented to each other when they'd decided to get together a couple times a week to walk the well-maintained roads at Laurel Hill, the dead people got the nicest views.

She fell into step next to her friend as they began their approximately two mile route through the park-like cemetery.

"Incredibly well, in almost every aspect." Except the writing assignments, which she was beginning to actively hate, but Tina didn't need to know about that.

"Oh?" She gave her friend a considering look. "Is this guy just whaling on you every time you see him, or are you sleeping with him, too?"

Bri sighed, but she doubted that there was any way that she could get her best friend to understand the differences between what she thought of as Bri allowing herself to be beaten as opposed to allowing herself to be disciplined.

Still, she felt obligated to correct her misunderstanding anyway, even though she knew it wasn't going to stick. "First of all, he doesn't whale on me, in any way, shape or form. Secondly, no, I'm not sleeping with him, although…"

Tina tugged on her arm. "Although what?"

"Well, he did bring me off the last time we were together."

"You let him do that to you?"

Her friend's disbelief was palpable, but she just chuckled at it. "Do you think that that was easier that letting him spank me? 'Cause it wasn't, believe me. They are both extremely private, personal events."

"I would think so!" They walked silently together for a moment. "So, how was it?"

"Unbelievably good. Just amazingly, incredibly good."

"Wow. That's high praise from you."

"It's well-deserved praise. I mean, even though we do have a time limit when we're together—"

"You pay for him by the hour?"

Bri nodded. "He's available for no less than a two hour block for each meeting."

"And that's how long you're together each time?"

"Yes. But I never, ever feel like he's rushing. He's a very relaxed and calming guy. He takes his time, and his profile said that he's been doing this for a while." Bri frowned. "I've never asked him just how long, though, but it doesn't really matter. His experience works very much in my favor, because he knows what I want."

"Did you fill out a profile, too?"

"Yes, it was very explicit about what I wanted and didn't want from our time together, and he's got an incredible memory, because he seems to remember everything about my likes and dislikes. He… he knows how to talk to me and what it is that I want to hear from him."

Tina looked confused at that.

"He's able to create a believable atmosphere between us —by how he acts towards me and what he says to me—that makes me feel exactly how I've always wanted to feel."

"Which is submissive, even though it goes against everything about who you really are?"

"But this is an aspect of who I really am, too, Tina. It's just not one I've shown to you, because that's not how we know each other."

"I know, and I'm all for people getting their freak on. I just don't like that this involves you being hurt."

"I know, and I absolutely understand how you feel—I do. But he's giving me exactly what I want and need. He's smart and funny and very caring and affectionate, and he's also almost solely concentrated on me. If my first sexual experience had been with someone like him, rather than someone like Sean McCartney, I might have spent my whole life exploring what I wanted sexually, rather than just barely dipping a toe into it now."

"Do you think you would have a better life if that had happened for you?"

"Not better, necessarily, just different." They completed their first mile long loop and were about to start their last. "And, yes, being spanked hurts, but it arouses me to an extent I've never experienced before, too, and that makes the orgasms absolutely unbelievable."

Tina stopped all of a sudden. "I want to hear more about that, but not while we're walking. What do you say we head out to breakfast?"

"I thought you were never going to ask!"

They met at a tiny place that was full of locals, where the prices were reasonable and they didn't skimp on the portions.

When they were tucking into their two egg breakfasts,

Tina said, "Okay, so what was this you were saying about your orgasms?"

"They're mind blowing. They're the kind that make you want to howl at the moon in the middle of the day." She lowered her voice and leaned forward a bit to say, "I screamed at the top of my lungs the first time—twice—and I didn't even realize it. He had to put his hand over my mouth and tell me to be careful of my volume."

Tina's eyebrows were at her brow line. "The first time?" she asked.

"Yeah."

"So he gave you more than one?"

"Oh yeah. I didn't keep count, but there were at least five or six."

"Jeez. Now, that, I'm impressed by."

"Me, too."

"So, how many more times are you going to see him?"

It was her turn to look surprised. "I don't know." Bri really hadn't thought about it in those terms, although she probably ought to.

"Didn't you mention that money was a consideration, or am I remembering wrong?"

"Oh, yes, it most definitely is, so I'll have to see what I can afford. But I have enough for several more sessions." She was already seriously disturbed to realize that she looked at the possibility of never seeing him again with more than a little trepidation and a sharp sense of loss.

Her objectivity—which, before she'd committed to doing it, she'd sworn to herself that she'd definitely be able to maintain if she did go through with it—was deserting her, and that could not happen.

Perhaps she should stop seeing him now—cut her losses before she got in too deep.

"Bri! Are you there?"

She shook her head. "Sorry. I was lost in thought."

"Stop thinking about those orgasms!"

Brielle chuckled. "It wasn't that."

But those thoughts did haunt her, even when she'd said goodbye to Tina and was back at her place, although she tried to shove them aside. She was only somewhat successful at doing so, as evidenced by the fact that she'd taken out her phone and booked him for three more sessions, which was pretty much all she could afford without canceling the trip the Europe.

As it was, that would be cutting it closer to the line for her—financially—than she'd allowed herself to be in a long time, but it was more than worth it to her. Then she put down her phone and sat down with her laptop to knock out at least one missive to him.

"Dear Sir:

I think the one I owe you first is the one about what it is that I fantasize about when I... well, you know.

And the truth is that, until recently—a year or so before I even began trying to find someone like you—I hadn't been doing that much. My sexual side was buried under years of ambition and attention to my career, and frankly, I didn't feel much of a loss.

It wasn't until I began to realize how much time has passed that that side of me began to make itself known again.

And, although I'm not trying to pander to your ego, what I fantasize about is very much like what has happened between us, although it takes place in a more romantic, less businesslike situation, with someone for whom I have feelings, and who has feelings for me. He's some nameless, faceless man I've been dating (I don't even picture movie stars or anything, never have, for some reason) and when we become intimate, I let him know that that's what I'm into, and, of course (surprise, surprise), it's what he's into, too! Who would have guessed?

And again, I'm not trying to butter you up, but the way he is with me is very close to how you are with me—attentive, concentrated on me, caretaking.

He ends up spanking me, in an introductory kind of way, because I'm not experienced in such things in my fantasies, either. It's very much like what you did for me. How I'm feeling at any given point determines where we are in the relationship—it's not always our first time together. Sometimes it's that we've been together for a while and its evolved into a kind of 'domestic discipline situation.

But regardless of what it becomes, he remains very loving and caring and focused on me.

Overall, I don't think that's too far from what a lot of women want.

Anyway, someone motivated me to want to get this done sooner, rather than later, so I did.

I hope you're having a good week.

Jenny"

It wasn't particularly explicit, and it certainly wasn't the "excruciating detail" he had requested, and she wondered if he might think that it was a bit lacking in details. But it was definitely what she had thought about when she masturbated —at least, before she'd met him.

But she wasn't about to let him know that he was now the star of all of her masturbatory fantasies.

And it was a response—and not a one line one, either. As much as she wanted to avoid another spanking like the one she'd just gotten from him, she found herself loath to reveal anything further, and she thought she'd satisfied the letter of his law.

Since she was already writing, she wrote the other one he wanted her to do, too.

"Dear Sir:

For my second message to you this week, you wanted to hear what I thought about what had happened between us the last time we were together."

Having written her topic statement, Bri sat there for a moment, thinking, before she wrote anything else.

"I'm not a writer, so I'm not at all sure that I'm going to be able to convey how I felt—feel—about what transpired between us when we met last.

The spanking was much worse than I thought it would be. I don't know if that's because of the fact that there wasn't a layer of cloth between me and your palm, or if it was a worse spanking because I had actually done something that was a misbehavior, which I think you know I am not prone to do. Perhaps it was a combination of the two.

Parts of me seemed to be quite enamored of it, despite how much it hurt—and it did, although I would have to say in all fairness that that was pretty much what I would have thought of—prior—as being a pretty typical spanking.

Frankly, I would go through almost anything to get to the aftercare. I don't think that I've ever felt so cared for in all of my life—except for by my parents, of course. I've spent my life alone, but my time with you has shown me that human contact—the kind you have so expertly been providing me—is something I want in my life, although I'm not at all sure that I'll be able to find any man who is quite as perfect as you are. Perhaps I am condemned to pay for companionship for the rest of my life, but I found that I would be much more willing to do that—or even to just put myself out there in the regular dating world—than I was before I met you.

How you've treated me so far is exactly how I envisioned being treated when, months ago, I allowed myself to fantasize about the possibility of doing this. At the risk of not being able to see you very often past this point, you are severely underselling yourself, considering your talents.

You're a Dom, but you've never been demanding with me—firm, even stern at times, but never just blindly demanding. Even when you've spanked me, I've still felt cared for, even though I know that that's not really true—I still feel it, regardless.

You've made me feel safe, and seen, and heard, and thought of, and—especially outside of work—those are things that someone like me doesn't necessarily feel very often.

Anyway, sorry to have become somewhat maudlin, but everything I've said is true.

The spanking was awful, but the aftercare was wonderful and the orgasms were... I don't think I have the words to describe them adequately, but suffice it to say, they were the stuff fantasies are made of.

Thank you.

Jenny"

When Bran read her messages—the second one, in particular—he was blown away, and he very much wished that he had her phone number so that he could call her. She had the ability to let him know it on the app, but she hadn't checked that box—he went and looked again, just to be sure she hadn't changed it, and she hadn't.

"Jenny, my dear,

Thank you for your thoughtful messages. I am sitting here both blushing and grinning like an idiot at your words.

I would have liked more detail about your fantasies, but I think I get the gist. Just out of curiosity, are there more details to be had, or is what you told me truly enough to get you off?

I am very glad that you feel so positively about your first bare-bottomed spanking, as well as what happened after it."

That sounded so generic, like he was writing a thank you card to his aunt for a birthday present. Well, not quite, but in that vein.

He didn't want to talk to her about how he'd learned to do all of those things for her by doing them with other women, but at the same time, he didn't want to let on to her that she was becoming very special to him, in a way that she shouldn't to someone who did what he did.

But he didn't have the strength—for the first time since he'd begun doing this kind of thing—to cut off contact with her. He wanted to see her at least one more time, he told himself.

He wanted to make love to her at least once before he said goodbye, but he couldn't write any of that to her, either.

"I had hoped that you might be feeling in exactly the ways you mentioned—in particular, safe—and I think it's wonderful that you've been able to get to that point with me on all of those different, very important levels relatively quickly. When we first met, I'm not sure I would have bet that you'd be able to do that at all, but you have, and that's all down to you taking an incredible chance, not me.

It takes a lot of guts for a woman to trust a man the way you have put your trust in me, and I will always feel humbled by that fact (and more than a little proud, not gonna lie).

And you're not the only one who is at a loss for words, believe me. My usual glibness has deserted me entirely.

I know it might come off as demanding or pushy, but I would very much like to make love to you the next time we get together. I hope that doesn't make you run screaming from me, but it's the truth and I wanted to put it out there and also give you some time to think about it before we meet again.

Your,
Sir"

When she read it, she spent quite a while staring at his last paragraph.

It was soon—too soon for her, really. At least, that was her gut reaction to what he'd said because that was what it had been all her life. But all her life, she'd avoided doing the same things she was doing—and thoroughly enjoying—over the past couple of months.

He'd said it before—if he'd wanted to hurt her, or worse, he would have done it immediately and gotten the hell away from her. He wouldn't have kept coming back to her and establishing a pseudo-relationship with her. He didn't know or have any real information about her, nor had he ever tried to ask. If anything, she had been the one who had been trying to pry into his life outside of their hotel room, and he'd shut her down fast, as he should have.

Before, it would have mattered to her a lot that he wasn't her boyfriend and that they hadn't met very many times, and they knew almost nothing about each other beyond what turned each of them on sexually.

Now, not so much.

She was comfortable with him. She liked him. She felt safe with him. And what was almost more important than all of those other things, she wanted him in that way. Bri wanted to feel him inside her. As boring as he would undoubtedly think it was, she wanted him above her while they were having sex. She wanted to be full of him, to feel him fucking her, and she wanted to see him experiencing the ultimate pleasure, just as he'd seen her.

Brielle didn't write him back, but she did find her mind turning back to what he'd said at frequent points—even during work hours—during the time they were apart. That was a matter of no small concern. Literally nothing else in her life had ever intruded into her work life, since—knock wood—she'd never had any kind of serious health concerns, she didn't have a husband to worry about, or kids to do the same.

But now, in the middle of a meeting, in the middle of trying to write procedures in regards to the merger, and trying to get annual reviews done for her team members, his face would pop up unbidden, along with a lot of very powerful feelings she did not want to be dealing with at work.

It was her greatest hope that having sex with him would dispel her need to obsess over him. Surely, that would be the antidote she needed to get her head back in the game.

Chapter 7

"HOW EARLY WERE you this time, early bird?" he asked when she opened the door, making her laugh.

"Only about fifteen minutes, believe it or not. Things are crazy at work, which means long hours, which means that crazy carries over into my private life. If it wasn't a—what do you guys call it? A bank holiday—then I wouldn't have been able to see you at all!"

"Well, that would have been a tragedy," he murmured, opening his arms to her.

Without the slightest hesitation, she walked right into them, giving him a huge hug. "Oh, man, I can already feel myself relaxing just hugging you.'

Keeping her tight to him, Bran said, "I think I read in some article that humans need no less than twelve hugs a day for growth."

"Twelve? Until you, I never got any."

She felt him tense at that and wished she hadn't said it.

When he pulled away, he took her chin in his hand. "Jenny, that is a very sad thing to hear you say."

Bri nodded, looking down. "I know."

He turned away from her to put his coat on a hanger, and when he turned back, she looked positively forlorn.

"I'm sorry. I should have kept that tidbit of information to myself. I didn't mean to bring you down."

"I'm okay."

He pulled her into his arms again, saying, "That's two," making her laugh, which was his purpose in doing so.

As he walked across the floor to the nearest occasional chair, he kept hold of her hand, tugging her along behind him until he'd sat down in the chair and patted his thighs for her to sit on his lap.

"So, your week was really busy?"

She sighed and leaned her head against his shoulder. "Incredibly, insanely busy. I don't think I worked any less than eighteen hours a day any day this past week, and it's not going to get better any time soon, either."

"Well, then, you are definitely due for a bout of stress relief, aren't you?" He threaded his fingers through the hair at the back of her head, bringing her mouth down to his for a deep, slow kiss that left them both breathless.

"How was your week?"

"Nearly as hectic, but— " He'd been about to say, "I'm the boss, so I only really have to do what I want to do." But he couldn't say that to her, and it bothered him that he'd been so close to doing it. He'd never accidentally revealed anything about himself to any client, ever.

Not good, he told himself. *Not good at all.*

Still, he wouldn't allow himself to dwell on it, not while he was here with her. He'd rake himself over the coals when he got home, not that he was sure what he could do about it, besides stop seeing her.

But he immediately recognized that that would only be a court of last resort. He liked her too much to— He stopped right there in his head. "He liked her too much" said it all.

"So, I noticed that you didn't respond to the message I sent back to you about wanting to have sex with you, Jenny."

She looked a little anxious when he said that, but his tone wasn't scolding, just surprised.

"Did I miss something? Did you say that you wanted me to reply?"

"No, I didn't, I just kind of assumed you would, considering the topic."

Bri laughed. "Considering the topic, you should have known that I wouldn't write back.'

He smiled. "That's right. You're my Miss Prim and Proper. Did I give you the vapors?'

"Just about."

"I would have loved to watch you read it."

"You wanted to be present for all of the weeping and wailing and gnashing of teeth?"

"I would have thought it was pearl clutching, mostly."

"That, too."

He put his mouth near her ear and whispered, "So what do you think?"

"I—" As much time as she had spent thinking about the subject, she still hadn't made a decision about it. So she said the first thing that came into her head. "I thought I'd let you decide."

"Really? Because you know what I'm going to decide, don't you, Miss Jenny?"

Her reply was downright meek. "Yes, Sir."

"Good." He stood with her in his arms, but put her feet on the floor before wrapping one arm around her waist and pulling her to him as he melded his mouth to hers. When he ended the kiss, he began to press very gentle kisses to her jawline. "But you are still—as always—charged with telling me if I'm doing something you don't like or want."

"Yes, Sir," she said, with more of a tentative tone than she'd had with him lately.

He surprised her by sitting back down in the chair in the same manspreading way as he usually did. "Sometimes I like to unwrap my presents. Sometimes I like them to unwrap themselves."

Bri stood their hugging herself and looking down at him. "Really? You want me to do a strip tease? Have you met me?"

Her discomfort was almost worth it to see the twinkle in his eyes as he laughed. "I think I might know you from somewhere, and the truth is that I know you pretty damned well."

That was the truth. He probably knew her better than almost anyone on Earth, especially in very particular ways—although she wasn't going to confirm it for him.

She continued to stand there, giving him a little girl lost, somewhat anxious look, and he had pity on her, relenting just a bit.

"You don't have to tease if you don't want to, honey." His eyes and voice narrowed. "But you do have to strip."

"In front of you?" she asked, sounding just as askance as she had at the idea of having to do a strip tease for him.

"Yes."

He heard her tsk in exasperation.

"What was that?"

Bri was more than smart enough to know what she'd done something she shouldn't have. "Nothing."

"That's what I thought. The peanut gallery should not be making disparaging sounds in regards to her Dom."

"Yes, Sir," she answered quickly, her hands already at the buttons of her blouse.

As he expected, the bra that was revealed when she removed her shirt was white and certainly nothing Victoria would bother to keep secret. Victoria would have burned it, which was something he would do, too, if he were ever given the chance.

If he were undressing her, Bran would have removed that first, but he understood why she went for her pants next. They were dress pants, and when she removed them, he hopped up and got a hanger, onto which he put her shirt and pants before he sat down again.

She was standing in front of him in her bra and panties that were from the same depressing (and perhaps Depression) era, and he was wondering which one she would go for next.

And it was what he would have predicted—what every woman seemed to move to after her pants were gone. Her bra.

Bran had always thought that that revealed much more of the feminine body than taking off panties did, since her lady bits were much better hidden than his man parts, and there was so much more to reveal in regards to breasts than female genitalia.

Not that he was objecting, of course.

Hers were—to put it politely—stunning. Full and round and firm, with nipples that he was glad to see were a dusky pink and already peaked.

Although she had hooked her thumbs into the waistband of her panties, she also cast a glance at him, as if she expected that he was going to give her some sort of respite. But she was wrong.

"I knew you were beautiful all over," he said, making her blush, which he could now see covered a lot more of her than her face. But then he said, "Keep going, honey."

She gave in to a little fit of pique and he could hardly believe it when he saw her stomp her foot in frustration. He let out a bit of a chuckle at that and got a glare from her for his efforts as she brought her panties down and off.

He stood again and took the hanger, from which all of

her clothing was hanging, and brought it to the generously named "closet" area of the room before returning to her as quickly as he could. Once there, he made a slow circuit around her as he looked her up and down, noting that there was a fine trembling in her body, and he was amazed that she wasn't at least as trepidatious as she'd been when they'd first met.

She'd come a long way, and he was glad of it, since there was absolutely nothing for her to be afraid of or worried or tense about.

When he stood in front of her again, her arms were crossed over her breasts, and she was looking at his feet.

"Ahem," he said, waiting for her eyes to find his, then nodding at her arms.

With very severe reluctance, she let her arms hang at her side.

"Good girl," he praised warmly, not that it made any appreciable difference, either in her demeanor or her shaking.

Bri wasn't sure exactly what it was that she expected him to do, but it was not what he did, which was to bring her close to him and kiss her, gently at first but then more demandingly. His mouth slanted over hers as his tongue found its way into her mouth, touching her teeth then dueling with her own tongue as she groaned softly.

"Lie down on the bed, honey, please."

Again, eyes that betrayed how hesitant she was, found his, so as she climbed obediently onto the bed, he made encouraging noises, like, "That's it. Sit down. Very good!"

Under her big, watchful eyes, he removed his tie, then began to roll up his sleeves, as he'd done before, and he thought he caught a bit of a gasp when he started to do so. That wasn't at all surprising. Many women found it highly erotic to watch a man do that, as it represented something that many men did before they administered whatever kind of discipline was necessary.

Then he stood at the end of the bed and said, "Hitch yourself up to the headboard, and lie down, please."

Once she'd complied, he crawled onto the bed after her, lying stretched out full-length next to her. In this position, the differences in their sizes was very apparent. Her feet were somewhere near mid-shin on him, if that.

Bran gathered her to him, so that they were facing each other.

"I know you're nervous, but are you okay, Jenny?"

"Yes."

"Good. I hope so, because there's nothing I want more than to bring you pleasure while we're together. I want you to try to remember that."

She nodded, but he knew that wasn't going to happen.

All of a sudden, he sat up, leaned back against the padded headboard, and pulled her over his lap.

Bri went, but she wasn't happy about it.

"B-but what did I do? Why are you spanking me?" she asked, keeping her head turned towards him as he got her easily into position.

And—naked as she was—she did not like how unhappy he looked at how she had questioned him.

"I'm sorry. Am I your Dom?"

"Yes, Sir," she answered quickly.

"And you've given me permission to spank you?"

Her, "Yes, Sir," came a little less quickly.

"Then you might just get a spanking when you haven't done anything—like a maintenance spanking. Or a spanking just because I want to give you one."

That idea had not crossed her mind. She knew about maintenance spankings—that's kind of what she figured she'd end up with, because she generally didn't do anything that would warrant a spanking, although he didn't seem to have a problem finding reasons to spank her. But to be spanked for no reason other than that he wanted to?

That was going to be hard for her to come to grips with.

It wasn't something that Bran did very often, so it wasn't something that she necessarily needed to concern herself about. But it got her thinking and worrying about that, instead of worrying about having sex with him.

His hand landed on her butt and she yelped, even though it wasn't a swat. But the next one was, although it wasn't anywhere near as hard as what she'd had to endure from him last time. It still stung—a little—just enough to let her know that it was there—that he was there, spanking her bottom.

But that wasn't all a few well-placed smacks would do for her, and that was what he was counting on. Bran kept them —relatively—light, distributing a few here and there that weren't so, but couching them between the easier ones. He'd seen just how excited she'd been when he'd given her a true spanking, and he was of a mind that to only spank her mildly wouldn't give her the complete measure of ecstasy that he intended for her to experience.

She might not agree with that, but she'd already agreed that she trusted him to do what he thought was best for her, and that was exactly what he was going to do.

Still, when he reached beneath her, to fit his left hand— with which he was just as competent as his right—over the area between her legs, letting his middle finger braille his way to a clit that was already soaked in her own juices.

"Very nice," he breathed on a groan.

Without really thinking about the consequences, Bri made as if to leave, and that hand came down on her backside in a way that had her gasping and whimpering as she settled back down again, right where he'd put her.

"Don't try to get up, Jenny, honey, or I'll blister your behind."

She swallowed hard, but her clit jumped at the same time. And what was worse about that situation was that she knew that he knew that had happened.

Slowly, over a reasonable amount of time, he built a fire in two places—her butt and her lady parts, one feeding off the other as her bottom began to sting reasonably badly, but he kept the edge off it by stroking that finger lazily over her pearl just at the moment when it was getting to be too much for her. She didn't know how he knew when that was, but he did—unerringly.

Eventually, he flipped the script and added his index finger to the mix, backing off on the spanking somewhat, but using a judicious amount of pain, every once in a while, to keep her right where he wanted her. She was deliciously, and surprisingly, verbal about her pleasure, and he was relishing every whimper that became a passionate moan, and every passionate moan that became a whimper of pain.

Her breathing was ragged, and she was writhing whether he was flicking or spanking her—it didn't seem to matter to her one whit which it was.

Then Bran began to rub the sore skin of her backside, while his fingers became more dedicated to getting her off.

"I want you to be a good girl and come for me, Jenny," he ordered, fairly sternly, as he began to spank her more often, and the combination—the use of the term "good girl" along with a command to come, plus the way he was spanking her, as well as all of the other stimulation—made her completely lose her mind, throwing her auburn curls back and letting loose with one loud, high note of a scream that she then bellowed into the comforter instead.

But he wasn't about to allow it to end there for her. Her body bucked and twisted and writhed and arched, and his fingers remained with her the entire time, forcing her to violent, ferocious peak after peak, until she began to beg him to stop, and even then, he made her come another two times before he stopped.

Once he did, he immediately pulled her into his arms, holding her plastered against him as he could feel her continuing to contract not just the area between her legs, but her entire body until the spasms began to fade away.

"Oh my God, honey, that was amazing!" he breathed down onto her.

Bri threw her arms around his neck and buried her head against the side of it, holding on to him for dear life, as the only safe place in her tumultuous world.

Bran held her tightly through it all, enjoying the feel of her—utterly relaxed—in his arms. At one point, he felt compelled to ask, "Are you okay, honey? You don't have to say anything, just nod your head."

She nodded her head, because that was all she could do.

"Good girl. I'd like to give you more time to recover, but I want you too much to do that," he said, by way of apology.

Before she had regained the ability to move her own arms and legs, he pressed her onto her back, reached down to free himself, and covered her body with his own.

Bringing her off was something he thoroughly enjoyed doing, but in this case, it also served a dual purpose. Her having been fully aroused would make it easier for her to take him. It still might not be all that easy for her—he wasn't a small man in any way. But he had thought ahead to putting the lube where it was easily used, and before he notched himself against her opening, he had slathered himself with the stuff.

"Jenny?" he asked, and it took her a minute to open her eyes. "I have to have you, honey. I'll be as gentle as I can."

She amazed him by reaching up to wrap her arms around him, and opening her legs even wider to receive him.

He was humbled by her gestures. Even so, he knew he was going to have a hard time holding himself back, but he would be damned if he'd hurt her

It turned out that he needn't have worried. She was tight —probably the tightest he'd ever had—but she was also built to accommodate a man, and at first, he took it as slowly as was physically possible for him as she stretched around him.

But just when he didn't think he could possibly not drive himself into her, she whispered, "It's okay, Sir."

He looked down at her, and she nodded.

"Go ahead. I don't think you'll hurt me—"

She couldn't get anything more out because he took her at her word, drilling into her until he could go no farther, and aside from a gasp that sounded more surprised than painful, she didn't seem to be in any kind of distress at all.

In fact, Bri brought her legs up to put them around his waist, opening herself to him even further.

"Holy fuck," he groaned, plunging into her once, twice, three times before he completely lost control and began to fuck her hard, but even that attempt only lasted a few strokes before he emptied himself within her on a long, low, growled groan.

She couldn't hear anything beyond the way he was panting into her ear, and she loved the weight of him on top of her, grabbing at him as he moved to one side and collapsed. She wanted to curl herself against him, but she wasn't sure if that might seem a bit too "girlfriendish", or clingy, so she didn't.

With his breathing still barely under control, and his head so that he could see her, he asked, "You okay?"

"Oh yes. Are you?"

He smiled. "I think so. But I don't have any feeling in my extremities in the moment."

Bri sat bolt upright. "Are you okay? Should I call a doctor?"

"No, honey, I'm fine. That's a compliment to you, not a cause for concern."

"Oh. Sorry." Bri felt like a fool for overreacting. "I didn't know that."

"I know. No worries." She sounded as if she needed a bit of reassurance, so he rolled onto his side and brought her to him. "Man, I wish I could go to sleep."

"Well, the hotel room is rented for the night if you want to use it," she offered.

He was already shaking his head. "I can't. Too much to do, work wise, but thank you."

"You're welcome." She thought—but didn't say—that she wished she could spend the night with him there, in that cozy room, but then he sat up, tucked himself into his underpants, zipped his pants, and then stood up. She felt ridiculous lying on the bed, naked, by herself, so she got up, too.

Pulling his coat on and grabbing his briefcase, was all he needed to do, and it was then that she realized he had never been naked. It made her wish that she'd brought a robe or something. Somehow, she felt even more vulnerable being naked with him now than while they were having sex.

Bran looped an arm around her waist and bent down to kiss her forehead. "You shouldn't come to the door when you're looking like that, all naked and well-fucked. So I'll say goodbye here, instead, 'Jenny'." Then he looked into her eyes in all seriousness. "You are an incredibly wonderful sub. Thank you for doing that with me."

Then he turned and headed for the door.

"Bye, 'Dom'," was all she could think to call after him.

When he left, she sat down on the end of the bed, realizing with a start that she could feel him dripping out of her, which was her impetus to get dressed, although she had neglected to replace the pads that she'd used last month, that usually lived in her purse.

She wouldn't like it—she felt unclean without a pad in that situation—but she could stop at a drug store and get some. Bri knew that that would drive her crazy on the ride home, which she spent on auto-pilot, reliving every second of their time together in her head. She couldn't have remembered anything about the four hours she spent on the road, she was so very happily preoccupied by what had happened between them.

Chapter 8

WHEN BRI finally looked up from the pile of paperwork she was buried under, she noticed that there was some kind of commotion going on outside her door. Streams of people were walking hurriedly by. She'd been ignoring her phone and her emails in favor of trying to make some—any—kind of progress before she was completely overtaken, and now, of course, she regretted having done that.

She got up and went to her door, opening it, hoping to waylay a passerby and find out what the scoop was.

Luckily, one of her friends—Rissa Chambers—was one of the people practically jog-trotting to wherever, and she reached out and pulled Brielle into the crowd.

"Where are we going?"

"Big meeting downstairs in the ballroom." That was what everyone called the enormous conference room that took up nearly all of one half of one side of the building, even though it was very rarely used.

"Oh? About what?"

"No one seems to know."

They were at the elevators, with crowds of other folks

who preferred to avoid taking the stairs. "Show offs," Rissa muttered as groups of women wearing sneakers with their business suits walked by them, as if getting sweaty before a meeting was a good thing.

"But, Riss, you're not 'no one'. If anyone knows the dirt about what's going on, it's going to be you."

Bri was not above a little judicious use of flattery in order to find out what she wanted to know.

"Well, the only thing I've heard is that it has something to do with the merger."

"Oh, dear. Do we think there's a problem with the takeover?" she asked in a whisper, as they crowded into the elevator with entirely too many people for Bri's comfort.

"We don't know," Rissa whispered back. "But it would be highly unusual at this late a date, I'll say that much."

Once the doors finally opened, they flooded out and—like salmon swimming upstream—they just followed everyone else to their destination.

There was another bottleneck at the entrance, though, because everyone was being given a new nametag, with what appeared to be the new company logo.

So, apparently, they weren't being herded into a room all together because the merger was off.

"What a waste. They don't even have our pictures, and they can't be used as badges. How many trees did they have to kill to make these, I wonder?" she groused, tucking the nametag into her pocket instead of putting it on.

But some brown noser extraordinaire at the doors saw her do that and said loudly, "Please wear your new name tags, rather than putting them into your pockets or purses."

Bri grudgingly took it out and clipped it to the lapel of her blazer—upside down.

Rissa followed suit.

They were kind of in the middle of the room as more

people poured in behind them, and Bri began to worry about her claustrophobia.

There was a small dais set up at the front of the room, with the big new logo displayed on the wall behind it, as the upper management of the company stood there looking highly awkward and terribly uncomfortable.

"I don't care if I do lose my job because of this merger. It's almost worth it to see Fuck Up Frank up there looking like he's going to be expected to take it up the ass at any moment," she whispered to Rissa, using the derogatory nick-name everyone had given their egotistical, lackadaisical, idea stealing CEO.

Francis Aaron Prout didn't like Brielle very much, and the feeling was extremely mutual.

It wasn't too long before the lights went down in the room, and a spotlight was focused on the dais as Frank moved to the front of the dais.

All eyes were on him, including Brielle's—that was until she noticed that someone had come in the side door at the last minute and was bounding onto the stage.

And when she recognized who it was, even though the lights were down, she very nearly sank to the floor.

It was Rissa that she started to lean on when that happened, and she bolstered her back up. "Are you okay? Is it your claustrophobia?"

"No," was the first thing she thought to say. She always denied any illness or weakness. It was practically a way of life for her and her friends. But as she turned her back to the stage, she changed it very quickly to, "Yes. Yes. That's it. I'm feeling very claustrophobic, and I'm going into the hallway outside to get some fresh air."

"Do you need me to come with you?" Rissa asked thoughtfully.

"No, there's no need for you to miss this, whatever it is.

I'll be fine, and I'll slip back in when I'm feeling better," she reassured her.

With that, she began to cut her way through the crowd, excusing herself under her breath. The rest of them were standing there, staring ahead like they'd been raptured, while she—heathen that she was—was doing her level best to get the hell out of there.

Once she made it through the double doors at the back of the hall, she bent over, with her hands on her knees, until she felt as if she could make it to one of the "decorative" benches that were strewn in every hallway, getting in everyone's way.

They came in handy for her at that moment, though.

She put her hand over her face. What the fuck was he doing there? "Dom" was at her bank? Why? Who was he?

Her mind was working on overdrive, so she wandered down to the door he had entered—by the dais—opening it just enough to listen to the very end of Fuck Up Frank's speech, which seemed to be some sort of introduction.

"So, since I've been bragging about my team to him so much that he wanted to come and meet you all, even before the merger is finalized. Here he is, Mr. Branson Kendall."

Even if she hadn't been able to see him—with his headset microphone—come to the fore of the stage, she would have recognized that voice anywhere. Although she couldn't hear a word he said once he began speaking. She was too busy trying not to throw up

Brielle made her way back to the nearest bench again, reaching for her phone, which, of course, she had forgotten to bring down with her. Without a second thought, she headed back upstairs. Once in her office, she closed the door and the blinds, barely resisting the urge to lock the door. She took a seat and started to look him up on her work computer, but then she thought better of it and used her phone, typing into Google Chrome—with shaking fingers that made her fat finger it at least four times before she got it right—"Branson Kendall".

The first things she saw, of course, were pictures of him in regards to the merger. He was apparently some kind of silent partner in the conglomerate that was taking them over —a usually reclusive billionaire that very few people who weren't a part of the upper echelons of the financial world knew anything about. He was famously publicity shy, so there wasn't much more than that on him, and the pictures were all repeats of the ones everyone else was using. Every entry seemed to be in conjunction with the merger, which seemed to have something to do with his family having once owned the bank at some point in the past, and that was why he was being so unexpectedly public about it. There was precious little before that.

Well, she thought with a sigh, it was a nice life, but she was going to have to find something else to do. She couldn't work for him, even in an indirect manner. It wouldn't be right. It probably wasn't ethical for her to have slept with someone who had anything to do with the entity that was absorbing them. She leaned her elbow on her desk and sat there with her hand over her eyes for she had no idea how long.

Bri could hear that the crowds were returning to their cubicles, but she didn't move. She couldn't move. Her life was over, and she wanted to take a moment—more than a moment—to mourn its loss.

What heartless beast of a person would deny her that?

There was a knock her door, just before Frank Prout opened it. "Knock, knock. I didn't see you down there, and I wanted to make sure that you got a chance to meet Mr. Kendall."

Fuck, fuck, fuck, fuck, fuck.

There he was, in all of his—what had she called it—"intimidatingly gorgeous" glory.

She had to force herself to get up and come around the edge of her desk, but she couldn't quite get herself to offer him her hand.

Luckily, he stepped up, looked her straight in the eye, stuck his hand out, and said, "I've heard very good things about you, Ms. Daley. I hope to set a time to meet with you in the near future to discuss the merger and what you think your department might need to make the transition as smooth as possible for the staff and, of course, our customers."

Bri was barely able to raise her hand, but that didn't seem to faze him at all. He reached for hers, squeezing the dead fish that it was gently, then releasing it.

She had no idea what she muttered in response to his platitudes. She was just grateful when they all left her alone to die in abject misery.

But he carefully arranged it so that he was the last person out of her office, staring at her intently as he closed the door.

"Fuck me sideways," she groaned, collapsing into her chair, but only for a second. She picked up her office phone and rang her boss, who, surprisingly, actually picked up.

"Yeah, Bri, what can I do for you?"

"Kay, I'm sorry, but my claustrophobia was acting up the entire time I was in the ballroom. Would you mind terribly if I left a little early today?"

"I don't mind at all. I'm sorry you're not feeling well, but I can certainly understand about how you felt in that meeting. Sardines have more room than we did."

"Exactly."

"But are you sure you want to go? Mr. Kendall is taking all of us—and Frank—out to dinner, sort of a get-to-know-you thing."

Brielle ran her hand over her face, thinking but not saying that she already knew him all too well.

"Well, you know how I feel about social situations, Kay."

"I do. I'll make your excuses. Feel better!"

She hung up the phone, muttering under her breath, "Yeah, you feel free to make my excuses to him. I'm going to go home and write my resume. Or consider very early retirement if I can swing it. Or jump off a very tall building. One of those, anyway."

On her way home, for the first time in her life, Brielle stopped at a package store and bought a fifth of the chocolate flavored vodka that the clerk recommended. Then she went home, got into her rattiest looking but most comfortable pajamas, put an order in with Uber Eats for a very expensive steak and an extravagant dessert, fed the cat—while mentioning to him that they might soon be eating the same food, so he shouldn't hog it—and opened the vodka.

She didn't have any glasses that were used specifically with liquor, so she grabbed a coffee mug, instead, and filled it to the brim, bringing the bottle with her. Thanks to him—who shall remain nameless for the rest of her life—she also knew to bring a glass of water into the living room with her, in case the vodka tried to make her cough to death, too.

Although she took a fair slug of it, it didn't cause her to cough up a lung. But she wasn't quite willing to throw caution to the wind and have a lot of it until her food had arrived. Once the door was closed after that, all bets were off, and the cat had better watch out for her, for a change.

While she waited, she brought up the app she'd been using to keep in contact with him and schedule to see him, and went to delete all of her upcoming appointments with him. That would mean that a tidy little sum would return to her bank account, eventually, whenever Visa, in all of its infinite wisdom, decided to return her money. They were damned quick to grab it, and damned slow to give it back, she knew from previous experience.

But he wasn't there. She searched for him, but he was no longer there. She even went so far as to do one of those stupid "in person" chats, just to make sure she wasn't hallucinating or something, or that the liquor hadn't gone to her head that quickly.

It hadn't. The person/bot/space alien on the other end of the conversation confirmed that there was no such person in their system. Bri wasn't sure how she felt about the fact that he'd deleted himself before she had a chance to delete herself. And it smacked of the idea that he knew who she was and had done so in preparation for meeting her at her place of employment, which he would soon own.

Then she deleted her subscription and her account entirely, wiping away tears as she did so. Bri also tried to find him on other sites but didn't have any luck.

Why hadn't she tried to pry into his life a little, especially at the beginning? Maybe she could have saved herself from this debacle if she had. She hadn't done that because she didn't want to think that he had done that to her, and look where it had gotten her.

There was a knock at the door, and she assumed it was Uber Eats. She hadn't been paying any attention to where her food was at all, or the fact that—since the plague—they had just been leaving it at her door for her to collect whenever she wanted to. She just got up automatically and headed to the door, like an idiot she would be screaming at if this were a police procedural television show.

"Thank you, man," she said, paying more attention to not letting the cat out than what was going on her front stoop. Bri started the sentence before she looked up, but luckily not before she opened the screen door. "Don't let the cat—"

"I won't let the cat out."

She straightened immediately, looking down at him in total disbelief. "What the fuck are you doing here, Dom?"

He had the good grace to flinch at her use of the name he'd given her. "I came because I wanted to talk to you."

"How did you know where I live?"

"Frank was very helpful. He gave me access to everyone's personnel file."

"I'll bet using that to show up on my doorstep is against the law."

He nodded. "I think it probably is, too, but I'm more than willing to risk jail to talk to you." He said it without the slightest hesitation.

And she shut the door in his face without the slightest hesitation, too.

"I'm just going to sit here on your stoop until you let me in."

"Good."

"So you're fine with me freezing to death out here? At the very least, my frozen, lifeless body will block your way if you try to get out."

"I don't know where you live, but I live in New England. I have an ice scraper, a fuck ton of salt and sand, and an ergonomic shovel. One of those things—or a combination of all three—will move you enough so that I can get out."

"Would it help if I said that I'm sorry? And that I had no idea that you worked for that bank?"

"No, because I don't believe you in either—or any —case."

She heard him sigh, and before she turned away to go back to her chair, she heard someone drive up.

"Fuck me."

It was her dinner, of course, and of course, he took it from the guy, who was just as happy to head back to his car.

Bri threw open the door and yelled through it like a fish-wife, "That's my food! I paid for it, not him! Why are you giving it to him?"

The guy just shrugged and continued to head towards his warm car.

She stood there in the doorway, while her screen door began to frost up and she could barely see the nearly freezing man on her stoop, as she put her head in her hands and started to cry for the first time that day.

"It smells awfully good, Brielle, and it's still warm," he mentioned hopefully. "Please let me in. I won't touch you if you don't want me to. I'd just like the chance to explain before important parts of me begin to freeze and drop off, and then I'll leave you be."

Damn him! She was tired and hungry and still very much in shock to find herself unemployed, and she wanted her fucking dinner!

Again, Bri found herself doing what she would scream at TV or film characters not to do as she unlocked the screen door and headed to her chair.

He came in, closing both doors and locking them behind himself before he turned to her. "Is there anywhere that you'd like me to put this?"

"Do you want the anatomically correct instructions or the shorthand ones?"

He smiled at that.

She didn't. There were still tears streaming down her cheeks.

Bran made his way to her kitchen on his own, since she —understandably—didn't seem inclined to offer any help.

When he came back to her living room, he stood there while she studiously looked anywhere but at him. "I just want to say that it is the absolute truth that I had no idea that you worked for that bank. You just said that you worked in finance. We met in Portsmouth, New Hampshire, for God's sake. How was I supposed to know that you lived and worked so far away?"

"Is that what you wanted to say to me?"

He had a feeling that if he left things like this between them, he would never see her again, although he couldn't see a way that things wouldn't end up like that between them.

"I deleted my account."

She didn't mention that she already knew that.

"I realized that I was developing feelings for you. That's never happened to me before. I was going to do what I could to figure out who you were, to see if you might want to have a real relationship."

"And you're a billionaire," she snarled, "so the chances are pretty good that you would have found me."

He nodded. "Yeah."

"How is it that you're a billionaire, and yet I've never heard of you? I know Bezos, and Musk and Buffet and Gates…"

Bran chuckled. "Well, only the first two out of the men you named are still billionaires, I think. The other two are busily giving away their money to good causes, which I do a lot of, too. And there are a lot of billionaires no one knows about. Not everyone is a publicity hound."

"Okay, so what is a billionaire doing hiring himself out as an escort?"

Bran was so glad that she was actually talking to him that he answered without thinking how it might sound to her. "It's… a kind of a… hobby."

"A hobby." She almost laughed as she ran her hand over her face. "Well, that's something I've never aspired to in this lifetime. How novel. I'm sure it'll look great on my new resume: 'obscenely rich man's hobby'."

That caught his eye. "Your new resume? Why would you

be writing a resume?"

The eyes that settled on his were rife with pain. "You don't really think that I'll stay at the bank, do you? Not that it matters to you in the least."

"Of course, it matters to me. I've seen your file. You've been there for a very long time, working you way up through the ranks. Your reviews are stellar, every one of them—even the ones that that idiot Frank did. It's not like I'm going to be there very much. There's no reason for you to leave."

"It's really none of your business, Mr. Kendall."

"Of course, it is! It's my company. I need to hold on to people like you."

Brielle sighed heavily. "Are we done?" She reached for the coffee mug and the bottle of vodka, filling it back up again.

"You're drinking?"

She lifted her mug towards him before taking a large swallow of it. "After the stellar day I've had, you're fucking right I'm drinking."

"When was the last time you had something to eat, Brielle?"

"Lunch was at eleven, Dom."

He frowned at her use of that name. "Your dinner is in the kitchen. Let me set up a plate for you. You don't drink very often, and you have an empty stomach. And if you're intent on plowing through that bottle by yourself, you're going to be riding the porcelain bus in less than an hour." Bran didn't really wait for her to say yes or no. He just headed back to the kitchen, found everything he needed, doled out small portions of everything except dessert, and brought it in to her, along with utensils and a paper napkin she didn't even know she owned.

"There you go. Eat slowly, but eat often, to counteract the booze." As much as he didn't want to, he took a couple steps away from her, clasping his hands behind his back so that they didn't reach out and pull her to him, whether or not she wanted him to. "I'm very sorry about what has happened, and I would consider it a personal favor if you would remain with the company. I promise that I'll do my best to make sure we don't bump into each other." He paused, while she continued to cry on her tomahawk steak and into her loaded jacket potato, and her three cheese macaroni and cheese.

Then he cleared his throat, because he knew that this was the end—the last time he was going to see her. "I'm very sorry, Brielle. I know you'll never come to me, but I'll always be around if you ever need me, for any reason."

With that, Bran headed towards the door.

"Why do you have to be so fucking nice?" she wailed, but she stopped, mid-wail to add, "Oh, right. British. You and the Canadians are two of a kind, with your sortilege and your royal family and your blasted caretaking tendencies…"

He had no idea what sortilege was, and he didn't know where the royal family fit into her thought process, but he was glad that she liked how he took care of her, and it made him pause as he reached for the door. "I like taking care of you, Brielle."

She was crying even harder now, and the plate he'd put on her lap was going to fall off it. Bran sprang forward and caught it just before it did. "That would leave a nasty stain on your carpet, honey, but you should have some of it."

"I liked you taking care of me, too!" she sobbed, and he ducked into the kitchen to stick the plate of expensive food on the counter and ran back to her. She'd curled herself up into a little ball of misery, and he knelt in front of her, wondering what he should do.

He certainly knew what he wanted to do, but that wasn't necessarily what he should do.

Chapter 9

"FEELING BETTER?" he asked, having held her head while she'd been retching into the toilet for the past ten minutes. Bran wiped her face, dropped the tissue into the toilet and flushed everything away.

"Oh, God, no," Brielle moaned. "Just leave me alone and let me die in peace."

He took her very forcefully by the shoulders and forced her to look at him, not caring if she threw up on him. "If I ever hear you say anything like that again—anything that smacks of you not wanting to live—I will tan your fanny until you can't sit down for a month."

Having him speak to her like that—in a way she knew better than to think was put on—sobered her up better than pretty much anything ever invented for the purpose could have.

She'd been wedged between the toilet and the wall of the small bathroom and struggled to get up from there, although she still refused his hand and did it herself.

He could tell that she was in more of her right mind than she had been, even as she bobbed and weaved a little bit while walking back into the living room. He followed close behind her, just in case she took a turn, but she made it to her chair. Bran sat down on the loveseat, as close to her as he could get.

"Thank you for taking care of me, yet again."

"James Earl Jones is back!" he teased, because she was hoarse from horking. His smile faded at the look she gave him, that clearly said that she wanted him deader now than she'd wanted when he'd appeared on her doorstep. "You're welcome, Brielle."

"Will you answer a question for me?" she asked, folding herself into the chair with her hand over her eyes.

"Yes, of course." He would gladly answer anything she asked him, anytime, anywhere.

"How did you—a billionaire—end up doing what you did for me?"

Bran sat back a bit. "I've always had—and this is going to sound really egotistical, but it's true—a way with women. Women like me. I was raised by a single mother who was very loving and warm and caring and supportive. And having had her for my primary example of how a person should be, when I was—naturally—like that with the women with whom I became involved, they really responded to it. And when I got into D/s, I seemed to be something of a unicorn because of it. I was, as you've pointed out so kindly, a bit of a caretaker, which, to me, is something every Dom should be, but rarely is. I've had my share of relationships, but when you have a lot of money, people—women—look at you differently, somehow. And I wanted to give other women the chance to have a good D/s experience."

"That's why you were cheaper than anyone else."

He nodded. "I had no need for the money."

"Then why didn't you do it for free?"

Bran caught her eye. "Because there's something to be

said for assigning a value to things. Free things are throw-away things, and I felt that what I do has more value than that, so I chose an amount that I thought was fair, that wouldn't discourage the average woman. I had no idea that I would become as popular as I did "

Bri snorted. "You think that that amount is affordable for the average woman? Boy, are you out of touch!"

"You managed to afford it."

"I had a lot of savings, which I was rapidly running through to see you. My best friend made me promise not to take a loan on my house or dip into my retirement to see you."

His face fell. "Whoever she is, I would like to meet her and thank her. If I had thought that you were facing any kind of financial hardship, I would have waived my fee."

"Considering what you know about me, Dom, do you think I would ever let you know that I was in financial hardship?"

Bran sighed. "Well, I fucked up in a lot of ways, didn't I? I'm sorry. I'd be glad to refund you all of the money you spent."

"Yeah, because I'm definitely going to let that happen. You knew me really well in some ways, but not at all in others."

"Not 'knew', 'know'," he insisted.

She didn't say anything to that, just stared at the floor. "I think you should go, Dom."

"Branson. Most people call me Bran."

"Most people didn't meet you as Dom." That brought up a question. "Has anyone else ever figured out your secret identity?"

"Surprisingly, no, but then, I've always been very careful. I've never ended up being someone's boss at a company I took over, either, in case you were wondering."

She was still talking to the floor. "You still haven't."

He sighed again. "Don't be ridiculous. You don't have to give up the career you built on my account."

"Don't I?"

"Well, if you don't want to work there, then at least let me help you find another job. My company could aways use more good people."

"What part of 'I don't want to work for or with you' is confusing you, Mr. Kendall?"

He would have preferred to keep her closer to him, but he still offered, "I would be glad to get you a position elsewhere. I know a lot of people in finance."

Brielle leaned forward in her chair, arms on her thighs, face in her hands and began to cry again. Only this time, it wasn't the loud, heaving sobs type of crying. It was much worse—the quiet, desperate kind that made him want to pull his own heart out of his chest and hand it to her. It would hurt less.

"I'm really, really sorry, Brielle. Needless to say, I would do anything to make it up to you, but it's useless to tell you that."

He knew he should go. He knew that she wanted him to go. But he just . . . couldn't quite convince himself to do that.

Instead, he stood, picked her up, and headed for her bedroom. He'd scouted out where it was on one of his trips to the bathroom with her. Brielle hadn't made so much as a peep for or against what he was doing, so he continued to do what he wanted to do for her, tucking her under the covers, kicking off his shoes, and joining her there to wrap his arms around her and hold her tight while she cried.

Eventually, the crying stopped, and she pulled away from him, as far as his arms would allow, anyway.

"You should go."

"No, I should be with you. I'm your Dom, aren't I? You

keep calling me that, and I still very much want to be that for you."

"That's ridiculous."

"No, it's not. What really need to change in your life? You don't need to quit your job. I'll withdraw my offer for the bank."

"What about your grandfather or ancestor or whoever you were honoring by buying it in the first place?"

"Oh, that was just a lark. An interesting connection to a bank I wanted to buy."

"I don't think you'll be allowed to withdraw your offer at this late date."

"Then I'll hire another CEO and not work there. I can work anywhere or nowhere at all. It's important to you to be there, so you should be. It doesn't matter to me." His fingers tipped her eyes to his. "What matters to me is being your Dom, Brielle. Just because I'm no longer on the app doesn't mean that I can't be your dom. I took myself off there because I don't want to do that for anyone else anymore. I know it's weird for me to say this to you now, but you're the only woman that I want to call me Sir. I love you."

Brielle could hardly believe what she was hearing from him. It was all too much. She couldn't take it in—finding out who he was, what he was, the sudden insecurity and instability, him arriving on her doorstep, and now lying in bed with her.

She opened her mouth, but nothing would come out. She couldn't even cry any more—there were no tears left. "I—I can't take any more. I just can't."

"You don't have to. There's nothing that you need to do, honey."

To his credit, he bundled her into his arms and just held her, all night. He brought her glasses of water, remained awake while she was in the bathroom, and welcomed her back into his arms when she returned. Brielle didn't try to fight him on any of it. She was too tired for that, at the moment.

The next morning, her alarm went off at five-forty-five.

"Son of a bitch," Branson groaned. "What is that?"

"My alarm. It's time for me to get up and go to work."

He sat up. "Okay."

"Okay?" she asked.

"Yeah. If you want to go to work, go to work. I will support you in anything you want to do. If you want us to live here, we'll live here. If you want us to live in Ibiza, we'll live there. If you never want to work another day in your life, I'll support you, although I'd be willing to bet that you'd get bored almost immediately, but then we'd find you something else to do."

"Stop, stop, stop. Again, it's just . . . too much."

Bran stood, and helped her up, too. "Don't think, don't worry. You go have a great day at work, and I'll be here when you get home." He hugged her to him. "If that's okay with you."

As hard as it was for her to turn her brain off, she thought she was going to have to come up with a way to do that. There was just . . . way too much going on in her life at the moment.

"I don't get it. You want to be a stay at home billionaire?"

"I want to be with you. You want to work at the bank, like you always have. Therefore, I'll be home when you get home. I'll go make you some breakfast and a lunch to take with you."

She didn't have the heart to tell him that she didn't have anything for lunch, because she'd meant to go shopping last night, and instead, she'd bought herself a very expensive meal that she didn't eat, and a bottle of vodka that she shouldn't have drunk.

But he surprised her. Breakfast was scrambled eggs, toast, and coffee, and her bag lunch was the leftovers of the meal she hadn't eaten.

"Have a nice day at work, honey," he said, following her to the door she was just stepping out of.

"This is so bizarre."

"I'll give you that. But while you're working, think of the fact that, when you get home, I'm going to give you a spanking, and then I'm going to fuck your brains out. Drive carefully!"

Brielle didn't know what she thought about what he'd said, but he'd given her an ear worm that came back to haunt her at various times during the day—like when she should have been working on the merger.

Her boss called her mid-morning, to find out how she was doing, and she barely remembered in time that she'd told her that her claustrophobia had gotten to her. She hated lying, and very rarely did it, for exactly that reason.

"Feeling better?"

"Yeah, definitely."

"I'm glad, because I need those reports before one."

Of course she did! There went lunch.

She shot an email to Rissa. "Lunch is off. Reports due. Sorry."

"NP," her response read. "Hey, did you know that the guy who's buying us—the head honcho—Bronson Something—has disappeared?"

"Disappeared?"

"Yeah. No one knows where he is."

Well, not no one, she thought. "That's weird."

"Yeah! He left right after we'd all trooped down there. Cut his remarks short and everything, left out of here like a scalded cat."

"Billionaires. Every one of them is a freak, like all rich people."

Some more than others, she knew from personal experience.

"Amen."

When she got home, never having forgotten for one second what he'd said to her on her way out the door, he greeted her there, taking off her coat and handing her a small glass of what she learned was whiskey.

"What happened to my chocolate vodka?"

"That's for college girls and people who have no taste, which is redundant. Sip the fine whiskey instead."

She did as he told her to, and she liked it. It had a smoky, caramel taste.

"Sit down and put your feet up. Have an hors d'oeuvres."

"Oh, thank you, I am starving! I didn't get to my lunch today."

"Why not?

"Reports were due to my boss."

Bran frowned. "I don't like that."

"I'm fine. I'm just hungry."

"Well, don't have too many of those. Dinner will be ready at seven." He looked at her pointedly. "And we have things we need to address between now and then, Miss Brielle."

It was strange not to hear him call her "Miss Jenny". But it was also nice not to have to remember to respond to that.

They were delicious little bites of she didn't know what, and she wasn't much interested in asking. He'd probably tell her that they were kidney or haggis or something just as unappetizing, and she'd rather not know.

When she'd had a few of them, and most of the whiskey, he took it from her and threw back what was left in the glass. Then he put his hand out to her rather imperiously, and she merely looked at it.

"Put your hand in mine, Brielle. Don't make me tell you twice."

Damn, she might not have forgiven him for his deception —and she hadn't—but her body didn't care one bit about crap like that. His still had an incredible voice, and he knew just how to use it.

Brielle looked up into his eyes, and—not without a certain amount of trepidation, that was very different from any of the other kinds of that emotion she had experienced on his account—rested her hand in his tentatively, as if she were going to snatch it back at any second.

But the warm of his fingers closing around hers soothed her quite a bit. "Come, honey."

He guided her to the side of her bed, where he bent her over, so that she was leaning on her forearms. Then Bran removed her skirt, slip, hose, shoes, and panties in an alarmingly efficient manner that left her wondering how many women he'd undressed before.

But she knew that wondering about that would just upset her, so she pushed the thought away.

She was left wearing her blouse and bra, and not much else.

He ran his hands over her flanks and her cheeks, embarrassing her by touching her and squeezing her in places that made her feel as if she were bought and paid for—when that was his racquet.

"Can I ask a question?"

"Always."

"Why are you spanking me?"

"Well, I was going to get to that, because I don't want you to think that it has anything to do with what happened yesterday. As much as I did not intend to do what I did to you, you are still the victim, and you are utterly blameless." He began to spank her as he made his explanation. "However, as I told you, I was able to peruse your personnel file, and you are just too proper for words, which has me worrying that you won't give me enough cause to discipline you on the regular basis I know you need it to keep you healthy and happy. So this is a maintenance spanking, which you will receive once a week, regardless of what other mischief you might get up to, which—apparently—is none at all."

It was—again—a different spanking from the ones she'd received before. It was painful, but nowhere near as much as the one he'd last given her. She'd never admit it to him, but what it was most of all was exciting. That big hand of his lingered just a bit longer when it came in contact with her blushing flesh, and when she had to dance a little in place— as he warned her not to get out of position—it was because she could feel her own honey dripping from between her lips, not because she was trying to avoid a swat.

And when he lifted her onto his lap and held her in those strong arms of his, she knew she was going to forgive him.

"Bran?" she asked.

He wanted to give her a look, because it was the first time she'd called him by his name, but he tried to be cool. "Yes, Bri?"

"I-I was worried that I was beginning to have feelings for you, too."

It wasn't a confession of undying love, but he'd take whatever he could get.

So he pressed his lips to hers, for the first time since yesterday feeling that things might just work out between them. "Well, Miss Brielle," he whispered huskily, "I'm going to dedicate myself to nurturing those feelings, even long after I hear you tell me that you love me for the first time."

Carolyn Faulkner

The words "spanking" and "discipline" have always sent a shiver up Carolyn Faulkner's spine. She knows she's not alone. Writing started as a way to explore her feelings. Soon short stories flowed from her pen featuring reluctant heroes taking the leading lady in hand, but always for her own good.

Today Carolyn is the author of dozens of books. She writes from her home in Maine, where she lives with her husband and leading man.

You can read an interview with Carolyn here:
http://www.blushingbooks.com/blog/?p=175

You may check out her website while it's under construction here:
http://www.carolynfaulkner.com

Don't miss these exciting titles by Carolyn Faulkner and Blushing Books!

Series books
Military Daddies
Lieutenant Daddy
Captain Daddy
Colonel Daddy
Major Daddy

Dangerous Love

Mistress Mommy Series
Alicia, Book One

Little Miss Series
His Little Miss
Little Francesca

Military Daddies
Captain Daddy
Lieutenant Daddy

Single Titles
Come to Me
The Gentleman Cowboy
Love Vs. Goliath
The Viking's Conquest
Second Chance Nanny
The Inconvenient Marriage
Promises, Promises
Love Cares Not
More Than All Right
Rescue Me
His Queen
Her King
Maddie and Daddy
Transgressions
The Brothers Rule
The Eye of the Beholder
Made to Order Bride
His Sugarbaby
Mr. Sunshine
No, Sir

His Runaway Bride
Undercover Sir
The Lark and The Bull
Doctor's Orders
A Babygirl for Christmas
Her Handyman
The Hart of the Matter
At His Hand
King of Hearts
True Desires
Lord Belden's Baggage
In His Care
Correct Me If I'm Wrong
Beauty Of The Beast
Tamed To His Hand
Daddy!
Amanda and the Stable Master
Lion
The Banished King
Northern Belle
The Cherished One
Forever Wife
Grace's Demon
Beauty's Beast
Captured by the Count
Male Order Bride
Sinful
Packed: The Enforcer
Submissive Love
A Heart Full of Heaven
Daddy's Girl
To Love a Man
Etta's Surrender
Her Secret Submission

Make Me
Let Me In
'Til Death Do Us Part
Promises Kept
The Obedient Wife
Old enough to Know Better
To Trust Her Heart
Naughty Girls: Brynn and Kim
After Hours: A Medical BDSM fantasy
Droit de Seigneur
Dutch and the Cowboy
Under the Lash
The Rogue and the Rose
Submissive Bride
The Unrequited Dom
Three's Company
All Hallow's Eve
The Reluctant Bride
His
Embraced
Attentions Throbbing
Submissive Desires
Kept
A Hard Man is Good to Find
The Spoils of War
Gilded Cage
Second Chances
Patriot Bride
The Boss of Her
Forever and Always
Tribute
Caged
The Substitute Wife
Captured by Time (w/ Alta Hensley)

A New Forever (w/ Alta Hensley)
Bound by Love: A Carolyn Faulkner Trilogy
Tears of a Vampire, and Vlad's Story, Two-Book Set
Never Say Never
Under the Cover of Love
Her Guardian Don
Her Knight In Faded Denim
Forever In Love
Depths of Desire
The Power Of Love
Only Her
On the Razor's Edge of Paradise
Indiscreet
A Most Unsuitable Mate
Make Me Yours
Ready For Love
The Gentleman Dom
The Supplicant
Belonging
Hidden Desires
Her Bad Boy
All Is Right With the World
The Error Of Her Ways
<u>At His Hand</u>

Holiday Stories
A Holiday to Remember
Griff's Christmas Angel
<u>A Season to Submit</u>

Anthologies
Tamed By The Cowboy
Blushing Cheeks Vol. 1
12 Naughty Days of Christmas2017

12 Naughty Days of Christmas 2021
Dominating His Valentine

Blushing Books

Blushing Books is one of the oldest eBook publishers on the web. We've been running websites that publish spanking and BDSM related romance and erotica since 1999, and we have been selling eBooks since 2003. We hope you'll check out our hundreds of offerings at http://www.blushingbooks.com.

Blushing Books Newsletter

Please join the Blushing Books newsletter
to receive updates & special promotional offers.
You can also join by using your mobile phone:
Just text **BLUSHING** to 22828.